DOVE AMONGST THE HAWKS

As a physician in London during the Wars of the Roses, Dr Luke Chichele became well acquainted with royalty and was part of a plot instigated by the Pope to find out exactly how King Henry VI died in 1471 in the Tower of London. Was it suicide or murder? The Pope wanted to prove Henry VI was worthy of beatification, while the King, Edward IV, claimed he had died witless and incapable. But the closer Luke came to the truth, the more his life fell into danger.

Books by P. C. Doherty
in the Linford Mystery Library:

THE MASKED MAN
SATAN IN ST MARY'S
CROWN IN DARKNESS
SPY IN CHANCERY
THE ANGEL OF DEATH

P. C. DOHERTY

DOVE AMONGST THE HAWKS

Complete and Unabridged

LINFORD
Leicester

First published in Great Britain in 1990 by
Robert Hale Limited
London

First Linford Edition
published 2001
by arrangement with
Robert Hale Limited
London

British Library CIP Data

Doherty, P.C. (Paul C.)
Dove amongst the hawks.—Large print ed.—
Linford mystery library
1. Detective and mystery stories
2. Large type books
I. Title
823.9'14 [F]

ISBN 0–7089–5997–0

Published by
F. A. Thorpe (Publishing)
Anstey, Leicestershire

Set by Words & Graphics Ltd.
Anstey, Leicestershire
Printed and bound in Great Britain by
T. J. International Ltd., Padstow, Cornwall

This book is printed on acid-free paper

List of Personages

Henry VI King of England 1422 – 1461.

Margaret of Anjou, Henry VI's wife and the most ardent defender of the House of Lancaster.

Prince Edward, son of the above two personages, killed at Tewkesbury 1471.

Edward IV, son of Richard, Duke of York, one of the most handsome, dazzling princes of his day. The principal architect of York's success against Henry VI and the House of Lancaster.

Elizabeth Woodville, a widow whom Edward IV secretly married in 1464.

George, Duke of Clarence, brother to Edward IV. A very unstable character, he hated Elizabeth Woodville and, because of her, went over to the House of Lancaster. He was later reconciled with his royal brother.

Richard of Gloucester, later Richard III. Trusted councillor, general and friend of his brother, Edward of York.

Bishop Stillington of Bath and Wells. A prelate and a lawyer, he served for a while in Edward IV's administration.

Louis XI, the Spider King of France.

Henry Tudor, later Henry VII of England: 1485 – 1509. He was the grandson of Katherine of Valois, widow of Henry V, and had a tenuous claim to the throne through the Beauforts.

Introduction

Fifteenth-century England was the scene of a violent feud between the houses of York and Lancaster. Its origins lay in the deposition of the last Plantagenet, Richard II, in 1399 by his cousin, Henry of Lancaster. However, matters only came to a head when the strong warrior King, Henry V, died in 1422 whilst campaigning in France. He left a young queen and a nine-months-old baby boy. For almost the next two decades England was ruled in the name of the young Henry VI by powerful factions of the nobility. When Henry VI came of age, however, the crisis did not pass: although Henry was a good man, he proved to be a weak king. In 1453 he succumbed to a sudden fit of insanity and ceased to be king in everything but name. The fortunes of the House of Lancaster would have been ruined had it not been for Henry's ruthless and energetic French Queen,

Margaret of Anjou. Surrounded by her Lancastrian warlords, Margaret tried to beat off the challenge to the throne posed by Henry's cousin, Richard, Duke of York.

The political tension between these two eventually erupted in bitter civil war. At first the House of York was severely checked at the Battle of Wakefield when Richard of York and one of his sons were defeated, captured and executed. The fortunes of the House of York now lay in the hands of Richard's three sons, Edward (later Edward IV), George, Duke of Clarence and Richard, Duke of Gloucester, (later Richard III). Edward claimed the crown in 1461 but not until the early spring of 1471 did he finally defeat the Lancastrians; first the Earl of Warwick at the battle of St. Albans and then Queen Margaret, her principal lieutenant, Somerset, and Margaret's only son, Prince Edward, at Tewkesbury. Somerset and the young Edward were killed, Margaret was captured and later sent back to France and, on the eve of the Ascension 1471, the hapless Henry VI, so long a prisoner in Yorkist hands, died mysteriously in the Tower of London.

To many observers it looked as if the House of York was established for ever (the only remaining Lancastrian claimant was Henry Tudor hiding in exile) but it had already sowed the seeds of its own destruction. In 1464 Edward had fallen in love and secretly married the young widow, Elizabeth Woodville. A beautiful but grasping woman, Elizabeth flooded Edward's court with her own retainers and cousins. Clarence, Edward's brother, openly detested her. Richard of Gloucester, more stable and secure, supported his brother though it was obvious that there was little love lost between himself and Elizabeth Woodville. The court of Edward IV became embroiled in a sinister power struggle which permeates these letters of Luke Chichele.

Luke Chichele's Own Introduction

I see the brother write this down beneath the date January 1491. He has two days. Two days the abbot has given both him and me to write my story down. And why not? The good Lord created the world in seven days, so why should my tale take any longer? Perhaps they are frightened that I may go, slip back into the black pit of madness, where the demons lurk. Great black shadows with the bodies of women and the faces of monkeys leaping and dancing above the flames. I have spoken about them to Brother George but he says they are phantasms of my mind, a sickened soul. I see from his grey eyes, sad and gentle, how he thinks I am mad. Well, why shouldn't he? I tell him I have lived in Hell but he replies I am foolish, witless but what does he know? I have wandered around Hell's burning streets, across its icy hills and I have never seen him there. So, what does he know? Not as much as I do. Murder, treachery, treason, men on fire with ambition, bodies gashed, public murder and secret assassination. The screams of the dying are carried, encouraged, pampered by the black ooze of treason, that's why I am here in this abbey on the edge of London, brought by King Henry VII's agents from across the seas. Henry Tudor, who is now King. The rest have all gone, shadows dancing across the fields. Edward IV, York's son, with his golden aureole of hair and ivory-white face, clothed in silks of blue, silver and samite. Oh, yes, I laughed when I heard the 'Golden Boy' was dead. His brothers too and the Woodville woman, his beautiful witch of a wife.

I see Brother George flinch at my words but who cares? For if I am mad, then it's due to grief. Brother George crouches over his writing-tray, shaking his head. A faithful monk, a careful scrivener, he puts down all he hears. Perhaps he is right. I rave on like a maddened wolf does at the golden full moon. Let me be calm.

My name is Luke Chichele, a native of Newark in Nottinghamshire, born in one of the not-so-great houses in the cobbled square under the tall, spired church. A stone's throw from the castle where King John died, his rotten guts running out like water after eating foul or poisoned fruit. I suppose that's where it all started. My father used to take us into the castle. He was a draper and the seneschal or keeper always wanted fresh cloth for the ladies of the garrison. Father, in his guttural English, for he was a Fleming born and raised in Ghent, would tell us about King John's death and take us to the chamber where he perished. My brother Stephen and I would stand open-mouthed in the room and speak in hushed tones about the death of kings. Poor Stephen! He would go home and pray in our garret beneath the eaves and beg the good God to have pardon on the soul of King John. God curse the entire brood of Planta-genets, be they York or Lancaster! St. Bernard was right when he said, 'From the devil they come and to the devil they can go.'

I was different from Stephen, spending the night wondering how and why rotten fruit could turn a man's innards to water. I used to go down to the fleshing-place, the shambles in Newark, where the butchers had their stalls. I would stand transfixed as the carvers slashed the innards of cows, bulls and sheep. Knee high to a buttercup, I would squat, ankle deep in the offal, not bothered about the orange blood or light-blue innards, the smell or the dirt but just marvel at God's unbelievable creation. Each corpse a world of its own.

I became a student, an excellent one, God forgive my pride. My horn book was always neat and I excelled in numbers and writing. My mother wept for joy, my father beamed at the very mention of my name, his thin, sallow face a veritable beacon of love.

'I thought so,' he would announce in broken English. 'I thought my boy would be clever. Flemish blood will out. Like his father he will go far in life.' And, ignoring the embarrassment of my mother and brother, down he would sit and tell me

4

for the hundredth time how he had once served in the household of Richard of York and his wife Cecily, the Rose of Raby, providing them with materials, samite, velvets, the best wool grown in England and the finest cloth woven in Flanders.

My father, a wealthy man, hired the best of teachers. I studied hard, learnt fast and entered the schools at Oxford, staying at Exeter Hall in Turl Street, the one built by Walter Stapleton, Bishop of Exeter. He had been Treasurer to King Edward II, until he was pulled off his horse outside St. Paul's, murdered, slashed and cut open like a pig. Murder. It seems to touch every aspect of my life. Brother George shakes his head.

'You must not do that,' he reminds me gently. 'Let matters unfold slowly like a roll of cloth being displayed by a draper. Slowly, carefully, so all the texture and colour is caught.'

So, after my studies at Oxford in the Trivium and Quadrivium, I entered the universities of Paris, Salerno and, finally, Cordoba in Spain. My speciality was not theology or philosophy, rhetoric or logic but medical care. I had read my Dioscorides, Hippocrates as well as John of Gaddesdon's *Rosa Mystica*. I liked the latter, although I do not believe a magpie's beak hung round your neck would cure toothache; or goat's cheese a pain in the eyes, or leeches the evil humours of the blood.

My real teachers were disease and battle, the great plague which swept the flat surface of the world with its poisonous vapour. Sweet Christ, I have seen the sights! Towns deserted as if pillaged by Death himself as he stalked the streets and stinking alleyways. Behind him the plague manifesting itself like some putrid rotten flower with its angry abscesses and black pustules. All life was gone. No crops were sold. No animals slaughtered and so starvation rode behind on its death-grey horse. In France, already ravaged by a bloody war, out of every wood and glen, people crept upon their hands for their legs could not bear them, to eat the corpses of animals lying dead in the fields. When these were gone they opened the graves and churchyards to eat the corpses of those who had gone before. Some blamed the Jews, God help that blighted race! Others, more simple, unripe cherries or the putrid fat of mutton.

De Chanillac, professor of medicine at Salerno, announced, 'The plague was caused by Jupiter sucking in bad air and spitting it out which caused the great sea near India to boil. Reptiles crawled out and spread the disease.' He recommended Theriac, the powder made from the chopped bodies of snakes which had been dead more than ten years. Other doctors maintained you should inhale over a pot of steaming turds. What nonsense! In Cordoba I found the truth. In the encyclopaedias of Rhazes and Avicennas' 'Canon of Medicine'. No one believed them but I did; the pestilence which walks in darkness and the sickness that destroys at noon-day comes from our own filth. Look at any house now. The floor is strewn with clay and rushes which are left lying for twenty years to nurse a collection of spittle, vomit, dog turds and other excrement. So, the disease will return. Brother George looks frightened but I tell the truth. I am a physician, no quack. I always remembered the epitaph of some poor unfortunate 'I died of too many physicians' and I came to hate many of my colleagues with their astrological charts and smelly urine jars. In my arrogance I wanted the truth and to be sure I found some of it.

I came home and joined the armies of either Lancaster or York as they moved like two swordsmen around the throne of England. One battle after another, bloody fights in misty valleys or in dank green woods. The same sorry tale, men hanged, cut, gibbetted. Sweet Christ, I saw the insides of many bodies. God's creation opened by mace, dagger, club, sword or speedy gallow, and I was there. I studied the folds of skin, the arrangements of tubes in the stomach and how wounds healed and others did not. Gradually my ideals fell away like a snake sheds its skin. My father died suddenly, hacked to death in one of those stupid little affrays between York and Lancaster. You see, he had never forgotten the House of York and when Duke Richard made his bid for the crown, Father, like the generous fool he was, gave him money and joined his armies.

He got himself knighted by Richard of York himself in the presence of one of his sons, Edmund. My father was with both of them at that battle in a snowstorm outside Wakefield when Duke Richard and his son Edmund lost the battle and their heads, which were later adorned with paper crowns and set high above Micklegate Bar at York. My father was no more fortunate; despite his plate armour, an arrow caught him full in the throat. His body was tossed like a rag into a cart and I hurried home to arrange the funeral. Memories. Black shapes against white snow. My mother arrived from Newark, her face and body throbbing with pain and grief. Stephen, pale, thin, already gaunt, even before he took his vows and entered the Carmelite monastery at Aylesford in Kent. My mother died within months, a second victim of murder, the assassin being grief for her husband. A good man. Oh, no, Brother George, not a saint, but a man kind and courageous. Christ, I still feel the pain!

As I said, my high ideals died with him. I became a physician, with lodgings off Rolls Passage in Chancery Lane. At first the other physicians laughed at me but my reputation spread. I insisted on cleanliness and used red cloths, draped over windows, to cure smallpox and so my wealth grew, one full strong box after another. I became well known in the city and watched the growing power of York. The Lancastrian King, Henry VI, I then considered witless, a fool, and openly admired York's three falcons of sons; Edward, later king, Richard, Duke of Gloucester and golden-haired George of Clarence. They seized the kingdom, smashing Henry's armies at Barnet and Tewkesbury in that hot, dry summer of 1471. The Lancastrian generals went into the dark, heads and balls cut off in some market place, and the Yorkist warlords swept south to London, a cruel horde of kites and ravens. Poor Henry VI died suddenly in the Tower but who cared then? I was lost in my own happiness for I had met my Blanche. Blanche Munnel, daughter of a merchant, skin as white as a turtle dove but hair as dark as the night; her eyes sloe black and lips like rich red cherries. Sweet as the honey comb she was.

She mocked me but she loved me despite, (as she often said,) my swarthy looks and jet black hair. 'More a Turk than a Christian!' she would pertly announce. Oh, Christ, I loved her and miss her still! Why are the best traps in the calmest places? The fiercest storms on the sunniest days? Brother George shakes his head. I am not to do this. So I go back down the tunnel of time. Blanche I courted, wedded and bedded. I continued to practise my physic, content in my lot until Michaelmas 1474, when I received a summons from Edward's queen, Elizabeth Woodville.

She had heard of my fame. I was to enter her household and receive rich robes and fat fees paid at Michaelmas and on the eve of Saint John. Perhaps a knighthood. I met the Queen in her palace at Havering. Christ, I could see how (even as a widow with grown sons) she had trapped Edward of York. Blanche was beautiful but Elizabeth was magnificent. Gold, red-shot hair, alabaster skin, a proud arrogant mouth which dazzled all the more when she smiled, her eyes dark wells of shimmering passion.

I took the benefits offered. I became a courtier, a man sought after, on nodding acquaintance with the King, his two brothers, the royal dukes; and the other great lords, Hastings, Rivers and Buckingham. Blanche was proud. We moved to a greater house in Lombard Street, the plaster white as snow, the beams of polished black; chambers and anterooms, kitchens and butteries and a long beautiful garden. I was there fourteen years ago, the roses were dying in the last golden burst of the summer and, although I did not know it then, so was my life. The descent into Hell had begun. A summons from the King. I was to attend on him in person in the great hall of Baynards Castle on the Thames. The letter was friendly. Blanche danced with pleasure, her sweet face flushed with pride at this further token of royal approval. I, of course, watched her, my chest puffed out with self-importance, my stupid head full of dreams, of being in velvet robes like some great lord. But pride comes before a tumble. But, oh, what a fall! Lucifer dropping like a star into the pit of Hades. I see Brother George shakes his head again. He says I have said enough. Let the letters speak, he says. Oh, yes, they have them still. I kept them, you see, in an old leather canvas bag, one of the few things I was still carrying when the Tudor's agents seized me and bundled me across the English cog at Dordrecht in Hainault. They have them all. Some do not concern this matter, so they put them away in an old chest outside the refectory door. But the rest? Oh the rest they have kept and Brother George will transcribe them as he thinks fit.

Brother George's
Transcription
Letter 1

Luke Chichele, physician, to his brother Stephen, monk of Aylesford Priory, all health and greetings. Another letter to a brother whom I never see but miss just as dearly as I ever did. Blanche sends her love and wishes you well. She does not like your order. She cannot understand, how ever strict the Carmelites may be, why we can only visit you once every three years. 'Too strict!' she cries. 'Too harsh for any man!' Yet she teases, for I know she wishes you well. I, as always, practise the art of healing and, I dutifully admit, accumulate as much silver in my strong boxes here, as you do wealth in the kingdom of heaven.

My service at court proceeds well but now I must hasten on to other matters. A month ago I was summoned by King Edward IV himself to his presence chamber at Baynards Castle. I went there in my best robes, expecting to be alone but, when the man-at-arms led me into that splendidly draped chamber, I found the King and my mistress, the Queen, attired in dress of state, seated in great chairs on the dais with a throng of people around them. In a window seat on the King's left, I glimpsed Richard, Duke of Gloucester, with his russet hair, white pinched face and green eyes, so glassy and hard they remind me of a cat Father once had. Seated next to the King in a glorious profusion of silk and velvet was George of Clarence. God knows he is a beautiful man, too beautiful, almost woman-like, with his golden curls and petulant mouth. The King, as ever, was in good heart, tall, big-boned, his great frame has filled out. Too much wine, boars' meat, and his favourite, sugared pastries covered with junkets of cream. I have told the Queen to watch her husband's diet, too much red meat flushes the blood and upsets the humours of the body.

The Queen was as beautiful as ever. A veritable Madonna in her cloth of gold and blue ermined trimmed robe. She smiled at me before her eyes slid angrily to where George of Clarence lounged, his arm on the throne chair, as if he would pluck it from his brother. There were clerks, scriveners, and other officials of the household. One man caught my eye, tall, dark, swarthy as a Moor with a finely trimmed, oil-soaked beard. He was garbed in costly vestments, the purple and white of a bishop; his white gloved hands gently polishing the pectoral cross which hung around his neck. Beside him, seated on stools, were four other men but their backs turned to me so I could not recognise them. A steward ushered me alongside them, a hush fell over the proceedings and I sensed there had been fierce debate and sharp altercation. I went on both knees and bowed, easing myself back on the stool. The King smiled at me graciously, as if I was a person of great import. He has that way with him. Of making small men feel great, humble men proud. I have not yet decided what I am.

'You are most welcome, Luke,' he began. 'My lady wife, the Queen, speaks highly of you,' he grinned. 'And of your advice.' He extended ring-bedecked fingers to the swarthy cleric standing at the end of the row of stools. 'This is his Grace, Pierre Renaldi, Bishop of Aquila, personal legate and emissary of our father in Christ, the Pope. He has come with a strange request.' Edward let his hand fall way. 'His Holiness,' he continued, 'has heard stories, nay, even reports, of how one of our predecessors, the late and lamented King Henry VI, has become the source of veneration, nay, even miracles. An appeal has been made to His Holiness and to the Cardinals that Holy Mother Church deem King Henry worthy of beatification.' Edward continued to smile though everybody else looked away.

So typical of our King. Nothing seems to embarrass him. For almost twenty-five years the King's father and family had been locked in combat with King Henry VI and the House of Lancaster. Both sides spilt blood in battle or at the execution block. Yet, Edward now took the possible canonisation of his former rival as if it was some great honour heaped upon himself. I, of course, like yourself, have kept myself free from the bloody whirling politics of the time but, in that quietened hall, I realised why the Pope's request caused such embarrassment to everyone but the King. Henry had been Edward's prisoner in the Tower when he died so mysteriously. Of course, I had heard the rumours. Most men say Henry died of displeasure, of deep melancholy on hearing about the defeat of his wife and the death of his only son at Tewkesbury in the west country. Others, a few, claim Henry was murdered.

The Queen was the first to break the silence.

'Who has made this request?' she asked, glaring at Renaldi. The papal legate raised his shoulders, shrugging noncommittally.

'Most Reverend Father,' she repeated menacingly as only my mistress can, 'I made a request. Who has petitioned the Holy Father?'

'We have had request from your own subjects, Madam,' he replied smoothly.

'And who else?'

'From Henry Tudor.' The crowd around me gave a collective sigh. Henry Tudor, the last of the Lancastrians, now skulking in penurious exile. He would do anything to embarrass our present lord and king. The Queen voiced this matter. Again Renaldi shrugged.

'There is more to it than that,' he replied. 'The Tudor claims a kinship with the late-lamented King.'

'How so?' Elizabeth snapped before her husband could intervene.

'Oh, sweet sister,' Clarence slurringly interrupted. 'King Henry's mother was Katherine of Valois. You may remember the lady, like many of our queens, had an itch between her legs!' I saw Queen Elizabeth's face go pale with fury, her eyes flash with anger and resentment. Edward's face too, had gone hard. He moved his hand and gripped Clarence's wrist until his younger brother winced.

'Continue, brother,' the King said quietly. 'But be careful. You can try our patience too far.'

Clarence seemed to heed the warning.

'Katherine of Valois,' he continued crossly, 'married again, a Welsh gentleman named Owen Tudor. His son, the Earl of Richmond, begot that nonentity now hiding away beyond the Narrow Seas.' Clarence stared at the floor.

'There are others,' Renaldi interjected hastily, anxious to avoid witnessing a confrontation at the English court. 'King Louis the Eleventh of France has also made a request.'

At this King Edward bust out laughing, throwing his head back in peals of merriment, lifting the mood of fear and tension caused by the altercation between Clarence and the Queen. The King just sat bellowing with laughter. Elizabeth glanced sideways at her husband until her face broke into a smile and she too began chuckling. Both rocked in their chairs, the tears streaming down their faces.

'Oh, Louis! Louis!' Edward shouted. 'What he would do to embarrass me.'

The King checked himself and looked straight at Renaldi.

'I accede to His Holiness' request, Most Reverend Father, all the resources of our kingdom will be placed at your disposal.'

'My brother, this is ridiculous, pure madness!' Richard of Gloucester slid like a cat out of his window seat. He padded across to the edge of the dais, his thick red hair flaring out like the hackles of a dog.

'For God's sake, my royal brother!' he asked. 'Why? Who cares?'

'Apparently, His Holiness,' George of Clarence quipped in reply, not even bothering to turn and look at his brother.

'I agree with Gloucester,' the Queen's voice interrupted them. 'Although there is comedy in this. There is, sweet husband, no real gain for us.'

'My Prince,' Renaldi interrupted firmly. 'My Prince,' he repeated and smiled at Edward. 'His Holiness the Pope has asked for an investigation.'

'On Louis' orders!' Richard reminded him. 'And so,' he sneered, 'are we to dig up his holy bones?'

Edward turned and glared angrily at his brother whilst Clarence bowed his head and sniggered like a girl. I glanced sideways. My companions, some of whom I now recognised, looked dour and slightly anxious as we waited for the great ones of the land to cease their bickering so we could find out why we were there to witness it. Somehow I knew there was little hope of preferment here. We had been called to perform some task, not to be advanced further. My reverie was disturbed by Renaldi.

'May I remind Your Highness,' he said, looking full at Gloucester, 'I am not here to advocate the holiness of any one, even that of his gracious self.'

Again the snigger from Clarence while the Queen smiled, biting her carmine lips with teeth as white and sharp as any fox.

'I am here,' Renaldi continued, 'As the Advocatus Diaboli, The Advocate of Satan.' The papal legate smiled and bowed at Edward as if the King was a fellow-conspirator. 'You know the process of canonisation. His Holiness the Pope always appoints a lawyer, popularly known as Satan's or the Devil's Advocate, whose responsibility is to find out why a certain person should not,' the legate paused, 'should not,' he repeated, 'be canonised. So, I am here, not because of King Louis, but to discover every reason why Henry the Sixth of England should not be canonised a saint.'

The Queen laughed and clapped her hands. The King beamed, his great face, framed by straggling gold locks, creased into lines of good humour. He patted the Queen on the arm and stood as a sign that all debate was now over.

'We have appointed a commission,' Edward announced, gesturing at us with one sweep of his great hand. 'Men of our household to investigate these matters and so help our esteemed papal legate in his task. Each is a Peritus, an expert in his own field.' He smiled down. 'Luke Chichele, a physician from our gracious spouse's household; John Ashby, priest of the chapel of our esteemed brother, George of Clarence; Roger Trollope, lawyer from our Court of Common Pleas and Matthew Gough, valet and squire from the retinue of our formidable brother, Richard of Gloucester. There is,' he looked down as the Queen pulled hard on the edge of his sleeve and bent over for her to whisper in his ear. 'Oh, yes,' he smiled, straightening up. 'And, of course, Simon Rokesley, gentleman of the Queen's Chamber.'

I heard a cough behind me and smiled as I glanced around at Rokesley standing there. He is a singular person, pleasant, very pale-faced, like some austere monks I know. He wears his hair short around his thin face so his great dark eyes stare out like those of a child. He always dresses in black like some sombre crow but, as I said, he is a pleasant fellow with a sardonic wit. A valet of the Queen's Chamber, I know him of old and I have referred to him in previous letters.

Nevertheless I should hurry on, dear brother, I simply want to tell you all that occurred. The King, now bored by the proceedings, stepped off the dais, hardly waiting for the Queen to join him as he swept down around us and out of the

24

hall. Clarence followed. I thought he was drunk. Gloucester shrugged, dismissing us all with one flicker of his hard, green eyes and went his own way. Renaldi also departed, though not before smiling and bowing at us in a most friendly manner. I heard the chink of mail, the royal guard of Knights Banneret relinquishing their silent vigil around the room which now fell strangely quiet.

'Well, sirs, are you to sit here all day?'

We rose as one man and turned to find Rokesley smiling at us, one hand on his hip, the other scratching the back of his head. I took the opportunity, while we all looked at each other, to study my companions. Sweet Jesus, and I mean no blasphemy my dear brother, but we are a strange party. Ashby the priest, small, dour, hard-faced under a mass of steel-grey hair; cold-eyed, ascetic I thought, looking at the thin, skeletal wrists poking out from the voluminous sleeves of his dark robe. Trollope, the lawyer, bald as a duck's egg, his fat face shining with oil above his fur-edged striped robe; his eyes were small and black, his nose slightly broken, twisted above bloodless lips. Gough, the gentleman, in his padded, purple doublet, the sleeves puffed out and slashed with white silk; on his legs were close-fitting hose of various hues pulled tightly across the groin to emphasise an enormous codpiece. A strange man, I had met him before. A good dagger and sword player, I had heard he had fought bravely in that cruel, bloody affair at Tewkesbury when King Edward had smashed the last Lancastrian army. His soldiers had followed the remnants of the force into the abbey there, slaughtering them in the nave until the floor shimmered with blood and gore. As I said, dear brother, a strange man and one you would not like; quite the popinjay with his crimped red hair, narrow face, painted eyes and the cascade of cheap jewellery he always wears about his person.

Rokesley made himself our leader and none of us demurred as he led us from the hall into a side chamber; rather dark, only one window high on the wall and that was sealed with wooden slats. At

Rokesley's bidding we arranged ourselves on stools around the long table. He lit some candles and the sconce torches before serving us with cold, white Rhenish wine. Rokesley had apparently prepared all this for he went to a small chest beneath the window and drew out a wooden tube which contained a roll of parchment. He unrolled this, using cups to keep it unfurled and brought a candle closer. His thin face seemed eerie in the flickering light and I caught the unease of my colleagues. Here, in this private chamber, so dark, even though the sun shone brilliantly outside. A bitter contrast to the bonhomie and courteous meeting with the King in the gorgeous hall beyond. We murmured amongst each other, introducing ourselves, slightly resentful at Rokesley's authority.

'Why all this secrecy?' Ashby growled.

Rokesley grinned, easing the tension, half raising his hand to calm other protests.

'We are a commission,' he murmured. 'A commission of royal officials appointed by the King himself to investigate these

27

matters. Now,' he looked down at the parchment. 'The subject of our investigation is Henry of Lancaster, erstwhile King of England. A man whom a few men describe as a saint, but many others as a silly madcap, a half-wit, not suitable to serve in the royal kitchens, never mind rule and wear the crown of England.'

Rokesley looked up.

'We must become knowledgeable about this man and remember we are not here to argue on his behalf, just the contrary. We are to prove the facts. Henry was witless with no claim to sanctity. We are to demonstrate this to Renaldi and, through him, to the Holy Father. In doing this, we show how Louis of France is being both meddlesome and mischievous.'

'And what about those petitioners from England?' Gough drily interrupted.

'Yes,' Trollope the lawyer squeaked; sitting next to Gough, he was nervously watching the squire half-pull his dagger from a sheath in his belt. A gesture also common to his master, Richard of Gloucester.

'Yes, I would like to know,' the lawyer

continued, 'who these people are. They are traitors.'

'Nonsense!' Ashby replied bitterly. 'It is not high treason to have a different point of view.'

'It is petty treason,' the lawyer shrilled in reply, 'to discomfort or embarrass the King with scurrilous slander and untrue reports.'

'Gentlemen! Gentlemen!' Rokesley's voice was calm. He glanced sideways at me and grinned. 'Gentlemen, we are as one in this. It is not our brief who petitions, but merely to argue on the King's behalf.' He jabbed the table-top with a finger. 'To prove that Lancaster was not fit to rule either here or in heaven. That is the important issue.'

Rokesley's words sobered and slightly frightened us. As one, we understood the bitter altercation between the royal princes in the great hall. Of course, the House of York had claimed the throne by stating Henry VI of England was not fit to rule. Now we could see the thrust of Louis of France's subtle attack. If it could be proved that Henry VI of England was a saint then York's claim to the throne could be brought into disrepute. I must admit, the thought frightened me. Once again, I was walking the narrow plank of royal favour. If my colleagues demonstrated effectively what is common fact, then Edward of England would not forget us. Yet there could always be a mistake. We could make some fatal error. I glanced around. My companions, too, had realised this. There was advancement here. Preferment, although I noticed Ashby was withdrawn, his face guarded. He just sat, staring at Rokesley, who sat drumming the table-top with his fingers as he let us reach our own conclusions. At last the valet of the Queen's chamber stirred himself.

'So, gentlemen, we are agreed. We all know what is at stake. So, let me refresh our memories. Henry of England was fifty years old when he died. He was the only son of Henry the Fifth, conqueror of France, and Katharine of Valois, daughter of Charles the Sixth of France. During his minority, for his father died in the first year of his life, the kingdom was ruled by

Cardinal Beaufort and a collection of great princes. As Henry grew to manhood it became apparent that he was a man born to be king but not fit to rule. In 1436 Henry became of age and, thirteen years later, married Margaret of Anjou. Even before his marriage the King's fecklessness became obvious. He practised good works but not good government. You remember,' Rokesley stopped at the murmur of assent which greeted his words, 'how, through him, the English crown lost all his father's conquests in France except Calais. How in 1450 his policies at home led to a most savage rising led by that dreadful malefactor Jack Cade. How the King was dominated by his favourites; first William de la Pole, Duke of Suffolk, and then Edmund Beaufort, the Duke of Somerset. So terrible were the cries for help from all parts of his kingdom that our present King's father, Richard, Duke of York, was, by the voice of the people, called from duties in Ireland and compelled to assume the post of Lord Protector.'

Rokesley paused and stared at a spot

above our heads, letting us absorb the history that he had described. I must admit my mind was not concerned with the doings of a dead king but, dear brother, with memories of our father and how that King's inanity had led to a war in which he was killed.

'About two years after York's return from Ireland,' Rokesley continued. 'Henry the Sixth became mad. No better than a witless idiot. At the same time his wife became enceinte. Many, however, believed that the King's madness was a sign from heaven, that Henry the Sixth and the House of Lancaster had lost divine favour. Richard of York, bearing in mind his own direct descent from King Edward the Third, laid claims to the throne. His rights were contested, not by Henry the Sixth, but by his wife, the She-Devil, Margaret of Anjou. York and Lancaster were locked in bitter civil war for the next twenty years. For half that time Henry was virtually a prisoner, witless, incapable. The real malignant was Margaret of Anjou and her generals. An evil abscess which was not healed until our present King's great victory at Tewkesbury in 1471.'

Rokesley licked his lips and leaned back as a sign that he had finished. Gough, who had been lolling in his chair, looked at the ceiling and sardonically clapped his hands.

'I thank you for the history lesson, Master Rokesley,' he said. 'After all, I was at the King's great victory at Tewkesbury. If that's what you can call the bloody senseless carnage. But, if these are the facts, what are we to do? Re-write fifty years of this kingdom's history?'

Rokesley shook his head, rose and went back to the small chest. He drew out a collection of parchments, all rolled and tied with red cord and gave each of us one.

'These,' he said, 'are warrants, safe conducts, licences to go where you wish in the King's name, on the King's business. You are to submit any expenses to the King's Chamber with, of course, receipts of any money spent.' He sat down again at the head of the table. 'Each of us will have our separate tasks. I will collect all such information. Ashby, you will look into the King's private life, his so-called good works, even the reports of miracles which are performed at his tomb at Chertsey Abbey. Master Trollope, you will study the workings of Henry's government, the effects of his administration as well as the legal basis for his deposition and York's right to rule. Master Gough, as a soldier, you will demonstrate Henry's criminal loss of England's rights in France, the devastation caused by his inept rule at home and how his intransigence, and that of his wife, brought about a long, bloody and futile civil war.'

Each of them took their tasks silently.

'And what about me, Simon?' I asked.

'Why, a physician?' Rokesley smiled.

'For you, Luke, something special. The Queen, Her Grace, she speaks highly of you, as do those in the city. You have a reputation of a skilled healer, an impartial man, even one of integrity.'

'I am grateful for the flattery,' I answered. 'But why am I here?'

'Simple,' Rokesley snapped in reply.

'First, you are to prove that Henry was insane. Secondly, being incapable, could he beget a son? Finally, you are to investigate the circumstances of his death. A few say he was murdered. My conclusion, and that of the Queen, is that either Henry died of melancholy or the evil humours in his brain made him commit suicide.'

At the far end of the table Ashby stirred, slamming his hands down upon the table.

'So simple,' he cried. 'We waste our time proving what is to be proved. But what happens if the story is different?'

'What do you mean?' Gough asked.

'What if,' Ashby replied slowly, 'Henry was a saint?' He shook his head at the chorus of protest, my own included. 'Forty years ago,' he continued, 'the English burnt Joan of Arc in the market-place in Rouen. We judged her to be a witch, a demon worshipper. Most of Europe, the papacy included, now publicly consider her a saint. The same could be true of Henry the Sixth only six years dead.' Ashby coughed and leaned forward, tapping the table with his hands. 'I speak in confidence,' he lowered his voice, indicating with his thumb towards the great hall. 'Out there we witnessed the bickering between the great ones and why do they quarrel? Not because some fool wishes to see Henry the Sixth canonised. Oh, no! We are talking about murder, the slaying of the Lord's anointed. I know what common rumour says, Henry the Sixth was murdered the same evening Edward and his brothers returned from Tewkesbury.' Ashby gazed around. 'And who gives the order for one King to die, but another? And who was in the Tower the night Henry died? No less a person than Richard, Duke of Gloucester, the King's brother.'

'Do not impute such crimes to my master!' Gough interrupted angrily, his hand falling beneath the table edge as if seeking a sword or dagger. He jabbed a finger at Ashby. 'Let us not forget the role of dear Clarence. Or shall we say turn-coat Clarence? Remember, he deserted his brothers and, for a while, fought for Henry and Margaret of Anjou.'

Ashby shook his head.

'I do not wish to quarrel with you, Master Gough. My main charge is that Henry the Sixth was murdered and now here we are commissioned to investigate his death and possible miracles. What happens to the small ones of the earth when they discover what the great warlords do not want to see? Aye?'

I sat and watched this little play of words and went cold. Of course, Ashby was right. What a morass we had walked into. I am a physician and I believe, before God, a good man. I wanted to raise no demons from the pit but, like Ashby, did not see myself as some marionette dancing to the tune of my masters. Ashby stirred and placed both hands on the table.

'There is something else,' he said. 'I have information, secret information about this matter. Harsh facts which will not make our task any easier.'

Again the silence.

'What is this?' Trollope stirred, twitching at his robe. 'What are you talking about?'

'About Henry the Sixth. I have secret information,' Ashby repeated.

'Where is it?' Rokesley asked quietly. 'Where did you get it from? Come, share it with us.'

'It is not here. I have it hidden in my house.'

Ashby bit his lip as if regretting his disclosure. 'Tomorrow,' he murmured. He looked around. 'My house is in Candlewick Street just beyond the Walbrook. Perhaps you can meet me there?'

'Tomorrow evening,' Rokesley interrupted. 'Just before vespers?'

Ashby nodded. Rokesley skilfully led the meeting onto other mundane matters, giving us further warrants, letters and a clerk's version, a summary, of the main events of Henry VI's reign. After that the meeting ended, each of us eager to be away, bitterly aware how the high hopes which had brought us here earlier in the day had not only faded but curdled, manifesting dangers on every side. I walked back down the long hall, deserted except for the shadows of the sentries, long and black under the flickering cresset torches. At the main doorway, Gloucester, surrounded by a group of henchmen, stared at me, his gaze unblinking whilst he gnawed at his lip and toyed with the hilt of the long dagger strapped to his belt. Gough went over to him, going up close, whispering like a conspirator in his ear. I saw Gloucester nod, frown and turn his back on me. I did not care. The night was cool, the darkness welcoming. I went down the steps, through a postern gate and into the dark cobbled streets, above me the winking lights of Baynards Castle and the faint calls of the sentries high on the ramparts.

I heard footsteps and Rokesley came up, slightly breathless, slipping his arm through mine.

'Luke, let us walk. It's good to be out.'

We did so for I was glad of his company through those dark streets. London has become an evil, sinister place, with alleys and runnels infested by beggars, soldiers now bereft of their killing trade, who look for easy prey and precious pickings. The pestilence had also just visited us, showing itself in ugly pustules, feverish sweat, aching limbs and blood-black vomit. The worst is over but still the bodies lie in ditches and houses remain sealed. The death carts trundle at night to collect their grisly burdens for burial in the great yawning death pits outside the city walls. One of these came by, forcing Rokesley and myself into a doorway and we had to cover our mouths and noses against the terrible stench. A great huge wooden cart pulled by four horses; their black manes hogged, eyes blinkered but their nostrils flared at the corrupting smell of death. Their hooves and the wheels of the cart were muffled so they glided by like some dreadful apparition. Torches flared at each corner of the cart throwing the rider into ghastly relief as he sat cloaked and hooded, a grim death's head mask over his face. Alongside him, similarly attired, walked his two-man escort, they did not even bother to look at us.

40

'The death pits are full,' Rokesley whispered.

I turned and saw his face white under its fine sheen of sweat.

'How long?' Rokesley asked hoarsely.

'God knows,' I murmured. 'Just be careful what you eat and stay away from dirt.'

Rokesley slunk further back into the shadows as a blueish white arm, straggling over the rim of the cart, brushed by us, then it was gone. We stepped out of the shadows, bowing to the friar, cowled and cloaked, who followed the cart, a lit waxen taper in one hand, his beads in the other which he turned as he murmured the office for the dead. Rokesley emitted a great sigh of relief and, arms still linked, we turned the corner, glad to see the tavern, its dirty blue sign creaking in the breeze, its door open so the street was bathed in the light of cheap tallow candles. Three members of the ward watch were trying to stop a fight between gamblers, their cups in the dirt as they pushed and shoved over a set of dice which lay on the cobbles, glistening white

41

like the bones of a small animal.

'Violence,' Rokesley murmured. 'All around us like a sea.' He stopped, stepped away and looked up at the stars, shining like diamonds in the gap between the towering gables of the houses.

'Simon,' I asked, 'is this commission dangerous?'

'I am not sure,' he replied. 'There could be danger. Ashby needs to be watched. Remember, he belonged to Clarence's household, and Clarence may be the King's brother but he is no friend. Men whisper how he hates the King for marrying the Woodville woman. They even say he wishes to be King. You have heard the prophecy?'

I shook my head.

'They say Edward will be succeeded by someone whose name begins with 'G'.'

'That could be Gloucester,' I replied.

Rokesley grinned at me.

'A silent one that,' he murmured. 'But come, how is Blanche? And you still write to your brother in Aylesford?'

He walked me to my door, exchanging banter before we wished each other good night and Blanche, beautiful as ever, in a red and white fur-trimmed robe, opened the door to let me in.

Perhaps that is what you monks give up, not marriage and the joys of the bed but being greeted by someone who loves you. Of course, Blanche was agog with questions but, when I told her, the disappointment in her face could not be hid.

'What is it?' she remarked. 'What's so special about a King they want to make a saint, when in life they couldn't give a fig for him?'

Ah, the wisdom of women. She flounced off to finish (so she said) a piece of tapestry. I followed, teasing and laughing so she softened. We shared a dish of bread and vegetables and drank deep red wine from the same cup and then, brother, we said our prayers and retired merrily to bed. God keep you and pray for us. Written 3rd August 1477.

Letter 2

Luke, physician, to Brother Stephen, monk of the Carmelite monastery in Aylesford, Kent. Health and greetings.

Since writing to you last, fortune has given its fickle wheel more than a sudden twist. The day after my meeting at Baynards Castle I rose early and went downstairs to break my fast, whilst examining the warrants and documents Rokesley had given me. These were the usual licences, writs and general letters demanding help 'for this King's good servant'. The document, which gave a brief chronicle of Henry the Sixth's reign, was no real history but, as I wrote last time, the jottings of some careless chancery clerk.

For a king who reigned fifty years Henry had an uneventful life, most of it dominated in his youth by his uncles and, later on, by his indomitable wife, Margaret of Anjou. One factor I did ascertain; Henry's first madness occurred in August 1453 and lasted until January 1455. No cause was given but, after that, he became a shadow of his former self. Henry died in the Tower on the evening of 21st May 1471, where his body was sheeted and taken heavily guarded to lie with his face uncovered in St. Paul's Cathedral before being moved to Black-friars for the funeral service. From there it was carried by barge up river to the Benedictine abbey at Chertsey to be buried; twenty-eight yards of Holland linen were used to shroud the body and money spent on wax, spices and torches; soldiers from Calais mounted guard whilst Dominicans, Franciscans and other monks were paid stipends to celebrate obsequies and Masses.

I threw the parchment on the table and went out into our garden to watch the dew dry on the grass and listen to the birds sing their growing chorus as the sun rose in golden splendour. I wish I had not been given this commission. I wanted to be back upstairs with Blanche or in my small room off the hall, mixing compounds, or reading the poor copies I had made of Galen, Hippocrates and Avicenna. There were patients I should see, colleagues to consult, accounts to be drawn up and certain interesting purchases I would have liked to have made from an apothecary, a Greek who had his shop down near the Steel Yards. Now all this was forgotten. The King's writ had made this clear. I was 'to put aside all other business'. I quietly cursed Edward of England; beneath his bonhomie and genial ways, a shrewd, crafty man. In the eyes of the papal legate, Edward had granted an audience, set up a royal commission, staffed it with men from his household, issued warrants and licences but, in actual fact, given no real help. We were to start from nothing and, in so doing, arrive at nothing. A gorgeously arrayed splendid waste of time.

I thought of the manuscript I had just finished reading and of Blanche still sleeping upstairs. I smiled, like any good doctor, I would mix my elements well, business with pleasure. I strolled back into the house, rousing my two apprentices from their chamber beyond the hall and into the buttery to summon the two maids. Young girls, ophans both, they work for us in the kitchen, pleasant-faced, ever smiling. I think highly of them but do not publicly show them much favour lest Blanche become jealous. I issued instructions, patting them both on the head, before striding back upstairs to rouse Blanche and delight her with the news. We would leave for Chertsey, spend time on the river and visit the great Benedictine abbey there.

We dressed quickly, I made sure my purse was full, placing a small writing tray in a leather bag whilst Blanche filled a pannier with bread, cold meat, fruit, two cups and a sealed flagon of cold white wine. The morning was beautiful. We left before the streets had begun to fill. The traders and their apprentices just stirring, making sleepy preparations for the day's trade. A group of soldiers wearing the royal livery passed by, whistling as they saw Blanche's face. She blushed and clung closer to me. I tell you, brother, I felt warm and happy and took a more favourable view of this task.

We skirted Westminster Hall and hired a barge near King's Steps, not one of the small wherries we sometimes used but a broad, larger barge, its poop and stern painted, with comfortable seats under a leather awning. The four oarsmen must have smelt my gold for they were courteous and civil even when they saw Blanche, minding their own business as they pulled lustfully on their oars. Despite the tidal change we seemed to skim above the water, under the roaring arches of a huge bridge. Blanche protesting prettily at the water boiling round us and turning her eyes from the huge poles stuck out in front of the bridge which bore the rotting heads of traitors. I spent the time pointing out different sights; the white greystone of the palaces: the different churches, covering our eyes as we passed the gallows, the bodies of river pirates still dangling there: the galleys from Venice, the huge fat-bottomed cogs from the Baltic and the great two-masted war ships of the King.

We reached the abbey just before noon. The barge sliding into the pier smoothly and evenly, the oarsmen bending, gasping and sweating over their oars, before rousing themselves to escort us gracefully up the wooden steps. Above us soared the great dark-stoned abbey, a mixture of towers and crenellated walls: outbuildings, granges, workshops and the small wooden and stone hovels of the abbey's tenants. Outside the main abbey gate I stopped a servitor, explained my business and showed the warrants. Do such people read? I doubt if he did but he saw the red wax seal and scurried away faster than a rabbit. A few minutes later the Prior came down bowing obsequiously, insisting on calling me 'Sir' as he led me through the monastery to the coolness of his white-washed office. I expected him to demur at Blanche's presence for sometimes monks are strict on allowing ladies within the precincts of an abbey but he seemed only too pleased, his eyes scarcely straying from Blanche's face. So interesting to note, dear brother, how monkish vows may prevent, but not suppress, the stirrings of the flesh. After he had served us wine, I explained my business and his face lost some of its good humour.

'The King,' he stuttered, 'or rather the old King. Yes, he was brought here some five years ago and now lies buried in the Lady Chapel.'

'Is the tomb often visited?' I asked. The Prior shrugged as if embarrassed.

'The Abbot,' he replied, 'should answer such questions but he is absent. Perhaps I should show you.' He did not wait for my answer but led us from his office, across the cloister gardens and into the great church where the sunshine streamed through the coloured windows like rays of divine grace. We followed him up the nave, turning left before the sanctuary, through a carved wooden rood screen and into the Lady Chapel. A small, stone altar at the far end, to the left a large statue of the Madonna and Child and on the right, under a canopy of stone, the square stone mausoleum of Henry the Sixth, with 'Henricus R' carved on the side.

'You would not think it was a King's tomb,' the Prior remarked. Behind me I heard Blanche move restlessly; already bored, she had begun to wander around. The Prior dragged his eyes from her.

'We were given little money,' he continued. 'We did what we could,' he shrugged, his eyes wandering away. I thought he was absorbed with Blanche but he was also evasive. I looked down at the stone plinth round the tomb. In the centre it was worn and smooth. I knelt down to touch its polished surface.

'People kneel here often?' I asked.

Again, the Prior looked away.

'Yes. Yes. We have fools who consider the late King a saint.'

I noticed the wax on the side of the tomb, smooth and deep. I smiled at him.

'Many fools,' I commented. I got up and looked under the stone canopy or arch above the tomb. High in it, on a stone ledge, were an old felt cap and a dagger-sheath. Ignoring the Prior's protests, I climbed on top of the tomb and removed both of them. The hat or cap was old and battered, made of expensive purple felt, the colour now faded, its fur edge ragged.

'What is this?'

The Prior coughed and looked down at his sandalled feet.

'Father, the cap and sheath. What do they mean?'

Again silence.

'Father,' I hectored. 'I carry the King's warrant. What are these?'

The Prior coughed again.

'The hat,' he mumbled, 'once belonged to the late King.'

'And the sheath?'

'That, too, belonged to the King.'

I glanced down at the sheath, the leather was yellow, battered with age. 'Oh, come, Father.' I said. 'That will not do.'

I saw Blanche, intrigued by my raised voice, come wandering back. The Prior licked his lips nervously.

'Agreed,' he said quietly. 'I do not want the Abbot or the abbey to be in any trouble but the sheath was left by one of the soldiers who brought the King's body here. He said it held a dagger which once belonged to King Henry.'

Oh, dear brother, how you monks lie! I turned away to collect Blanche and made ready to leave Chertsey. The journey had not been without profit: the tomb of King Henry was a source of pilgrimage, the smoothness of the plinth and the heavy coating of wax over the tomb proved this. The sheath, which I had thrust back into the Prior's hand, might also provide another version of King Henry's death. The Prior, I surmised, was lying. Henry the Sixth had detested all weapons. Did the sheath once hold the dagger which killed the old King? Perhaps King Henry did not die of melancholy.

We were already out of the church when the Prior, breathless, caught up with us.

'Master Luke,' he gasped. 'There will be no trouble?' I had hoped the Prior would follow us.

'There will be no trouble,' I said, 'provided you give me the name of the soldier who brought the sheath.' I held up my right hand. 'I swear there will be no trouble. Do not say you do not have the name. I know the rules of your house,' I lied. 'The sheath is a gift and the Rule of Saint Benedict quite clearly states that the donor's name is to be inscribed on some monastic roll.' I steeled myself against the panic in the monk's eyes. 'Please,' I added, 'give me the name.'

The Prior was about to protest but thought better of it and hurried away. Blanche and I sat on the cloister wall. We must have waited a full half-hour, chatting and enjoying the sun and the faint, sweet song of the birds. At last the Prior returned to thrust a scrap of parchment into my hands. I rose, bade him a graceful farewell and went back to rejoin the barge.

We arrived back at Westminster late in the afternoon. Blanche, now tired, went immediately home whilst I made my way up to the Walbrook and Ashby's house. A two-storied stone and timber affair, narrowly wedged between two great warehouses: the windows were shuttered, the main door barred. Along one side of the house ran a small alleyway. When I looked down it, the gate, presumably leading to a garden, also seemed locked. I went back to the front door and beat heartily upon it. No answer. The bells of

St. Paul's boomed out, the signal for the beginning of vespers. I looked around but the street was narrow, empty, a quiet place. I wondered where the others were and jumped as Rokesley came silently behind me and tapped me on the shoulder.

'What is the matter, Luke?'

I told him and, taking the dagger from his belt, Rokesley also pounded on the door. Gough and Trollope now joined us and, at their suggestion, we went back down the narrow alleyway, the gate at the end, surprisingly enough, was now slightly open. We pushed it back and entered a long garden with raised flower beds, all enclosed by a high, yellow, stone wall. At the far end I caught the glimpse of water and tall, narrow lily stems.

'What is that?' I asked.

Rokesley looked over the flower bed.

'Ashby's stew, or carp pond,' he commented. 'But where is the fellow?'

I climbed on to one of the flower beds and looked around the garden, jumping down in alarm at what I saw, a flash of colour floating in the pond. I ran as fast as I could along the narrow twisting path. The carp pond was huge, the water cold, icy to the touch and in the middle, floating face down amongst the lilies, was Ashby the priest. Followed by Rokesley, I waded into the water and pulled out the clothed corpse, made all the heavier by its water-drenched robes. No accident, the garrotte string around his neck was still there, tight, twisting, biting into the soft skin of the throat. The face a blueish white, the swollen tongue caught between the teeth, the eyes protuberant, rolled back, staring emptily up at the sky.

We dragged the corpse across the grass, the place seemed to lose its sunlight, the fresh fragrance of its white-faced flowers, even the birdsong died. We just stood around the corpse until Rokesley stirred himself, despatching Trollope to send a messenger, anyone, to the local alderman and, if possible, the city coroner. Once done, he led us back into the house to wait in the small, lime-painted buttery. I picked up the cup of mulled wine, still warm, which Ashby must have taken out to the garden and left on the edge of the seat. I poured the wine out and placed it on the table. We were still sitting there when the coroner arrived; our conversation nothing but meaningless phrases about how it could happen, bemoaning the violence of the time, yet, secretly, we all sensed the truth. Ashby had been murdered, not for gain, but, God knows why, for some mysterious reason connected with the task entrusted to all of us.

I volunteered to take the coroner and the two lay brothers accompanying him back out into the garden to examine Ashby's body before it was wrapped in canvas and unceremoniously hoisted up by the two lay brothers who chatted about the price of onions as they took the corpse out to the waiting cart. Just before they closed the leather flaps over the corpse I caught one last glimpse of Ashby's blue-white face, lolling tongue and staring eyes. They reminded me of the carp which had been playfully nudging the body when we pulled it out of the water. Ashby's soul was gone but who was the assassin? Back in the house Gough still lounged upon the kitchen bench, his cat eyes closed as if asleep whilst Rokesley and Trollope comforted an old hag, hysterical with sobbing. Their efforts met with little success so I pushed them aside and took her by the hand.

'What is your name?' I asked, guiding her back to the stool. She slumped down like a half-empty sack, flouncing out her dusty, grey skirt with trembling, blue-veined hands.

'Agnes,' she sobbed, her red, rheumy eyes awash with tears. 'He, Master Ashby, sent me out today,' she wailed. 'He sent me out. Told me to go up to the Shambles near Newgate, said he had business to attend to before his visitors came.'

'What business?' I interrupted.

She shook her head.

'I don't know. He seemed withdrawn. He had been for weeks but even more so today.' She gazed up at me. 'I live here in the garret at the top of the stairs.' She smirked. 'Being a priest, Master Ashby had to be careful of his reputation.' She opened her red, sore-gummed mouth. 'No one could accuse me of being his concubine.'

'Did you notice anything untoward?' Trollope interrupted. 'Anything?'

'He was withdrawn,' the crone repeated. 'At night he would sit here. Here or in the hall. I saw him once, candles burning around him as he studied some documents.'

'Where are they?' Gough asked impatiently. 'Let us search the house. Who knows, the murderer may still be here. Perhaps that's why he came, for those documents. Come!'

'No, you cannot.'

We turned, the coroner stood in the doorway like the figure of death with his bald head, watery eyes and ever-dripping nose. His raised hands clawed the air like those of a bird as he talked to us.

'You cannot go round here,' he added pompously. 'There is no mark of disturbance. Apart from the old crone's garret, all rooms, coffers, chests, will be sealed by my office.' The coroner turned and called out behind him. A big, burly fellow appeared, red-haired, craggy-faced, but he moved as delicately as a nun. Again the coroner's hand clawed the air.

'While you have been gossiping here, my secretarius has already been round this house.' He smiled at us. 'Nothing has been disturbed and nothing will be.'

Rokesley walked aggressively towards him, pulling the King's warrant from his wallet. The coroner's eyes narrowed.

'Who are you?' he said. 'Yes, who are you people?' he snapped. 'Why are you here?'

Rokesley thrust the warrant before his eyes.

'The King's business. The King's warrant,' he said. 'No, master coroner, you will seal nothing. You have the body. Summon a jury. Determine the cause but get out!'

The coroner glared at Rokesley.

'This place is sealed!' he snapped back and swept through the kitchen, clicking his fingers at the secretarius to attend him. I followed both of them out.

'Sir!' I called. The coroner spun round, his face suffused with anger. 'I apologise,' I said meekly, glad to see the hard eyes soften. 'I apologise.'

The man nodded.

'And your name, sir?'

I told him and his face broke into the nearest resemblance to a smile.

'I will not forget your courtesy, sir,' he replied and stalked out of the house.

Personally, I couldn't stand the fellow but I was intrigued by Ashby's death and could see no point in making an enemy of someone we might later need. All doctors are time-servers, my dear brother, and I am no different. Moreover, I was selfish. Whoever killed Ashby might have equally similar designs on myself.

I rejoined my colleagues in the kitchen where we sat like schoolboys round the rough hewn table.

'Ashby was murdered!' Trollope began. 'Let us forget the hypocrisy and the pretence. He was murdered because of what he told us yesterday.' He stared round at all of us. 'Only we here knew about our visit, the time and the circumstances. One of us must be the murderer!'

I looked with interest at this cunning, shrewd lawyer; sharper, more incisive than I thought behind the squeaky voice and diffident manner.

'As I said, one of us,' he continued. 'But who? Where were we all?' He looked at me. 'You are the physician, Master Luke. How long had Ashby been dead?'

I remembered the icy, fish-like skin.

'Two or three hours ago,' I murmured.

'I was at the inns of court,' the lawyer snapped. 'And you, master physician?'

'At Chertsey, with my wife.'

'Master Gough?'

The squire moved lazily, like a cat.

'Why should I account to you? I answer to Duke Richard and was busy on his affairs.'

'Come,' Rokesley brusquely intervened. 'Let us be honest. First, we do not know what Ashby told other people. Secondly, others knew of our commission and, finally, Ashby spoke in the royal palace where the very walls have ears.'

Quietly I agreed with Rokesley but something rankled, deep in my mind, something was wrong. It bothered me then and still does. After that our meeting broke up. Rokesley telling us to go about our duties but he took me aside.

'Luke,' he murmured, his eyes anxious, his face strained. 'The lawyer was right, the murderer could well be one of us. But let's leave his death to the coroner. I ask you one favour. Would you take over Ashby's brief in the commission? Where possible, try and investigate the so-called sanctity of Henry's life?'

My mind went back to that lonely tomb at Chertsey. I nodded agreement and he let me go.

The sun was setting. I walked back up the deserted streets, jumping aside as a party of horsemen, wearing the White Boar rampant of Richard of Gloucester, clattered by. Dressed in full armour, their helmets strapped to their saddle bows, I watched them go and wondered why the Duke had brought armed men to the city. I admit, brother, I was frightened, standing in that deserted street, locked, trapped in circles of deceit, treachery and murder. A King who may have been a fool or a saint. A prince who died through the failing humours of his mind. Or had he been brutally murdered? A priest who knew secrets but had his life choked out before he could talk and, on the dark edge of the circle, the great lords of the land, with their hosts of armoured men, rank after rank of mailed death. I was pleased to get home. Blanche was waiting for me, still full of her visit up the river but she became crestfallen and subdued by my silence and evasive answers. We sat apart, she working on some embroidery while I examined my collection of ancient coins. Each in its small velvet bag, the legacy of Empire, the gold of Caesars. All would have their stories. Who had held them? What had they bought? And why had they been dropped in the mudflats along the Thames? In any age gold can buy power, glory even lives. My mind returned to Ashby and, still vexed at heart, I cleared the coins away and went to bed.

The next morning I decided, before working on the King's task, to visit a plague house nearby. I resented being taken from my calling and, in my melancholy, preferred to visit the place, not really caring about the great red cross daubed on the door. Once a happy home of a journeyman, skilled in the treating of cloth, two people had died there a month previous. So, the house had been locked, its inmates prisoners, passers-by warned off by the great scarlet cross and the two guards placed there. I despised them, city thugs, rifflers, roaring boys hiding behind the livery of the city. I showed these my warrant as a doctor and went up to one of the windows, my knuckles rapping hard on its wooden slats. They swung open to reveal a pitiful scene. The journeyman and his wife, their faces white, hair straggling and sweat-soaked, looked out.

'For God's sake, Master Luke,' the man croaked. 'Our water is now brackish and what provender we have is almost exhausted. We followed your advice, the pestilence has not re-appeared.'

Behind him I heard the soul-wrenching cry of a child and that was enough. I returned to the two thugs who guarded the house.

'Open the door!' I ordered. They were about to refuse so I pulled out one of the warrants given to me for the King's commission. The fools would not know the difference and, when they saw the red royal seal, they undid the padlock and lifted the bar. I pushed the door open and went inside. The house smelt musty, though I smiled as I caught the faint fragrance of lime. The journeyman had followed my instructions, removing all rubbish out into the streets. This included the jakes box which I had also ordered to be regularly coated with lime. The family, however, were a pitiful sight and I was only too pleased to use pen and parchment and, finding a bit of wax, softened it, sealing my letter with the physician's mark. The warrant now declared the house free of the pestilence and the journeyman had every right to go where he wished and resume his trade. I gave them some silver, I don't know why, I thought of you, Stephen, the luxuries of my own life and I felt guilty, the money helped to take my shame away. I had a further row with the two thugs but again, money changed hands, and they became sweeter, promising to scrub the red cross off and inform the alderman that the house was now judged free of the pestilence.

I watched them swagger off and made my way down Thames Street towards Westminster, busy as ever. Remember, I took you there? Constantly humming and buzzing like an overturned beehive. The lawyers, serjeants-at-arms, judges, tip-staffs, each with their fur-trimmed robes and badges of office. A line of felons cruelly chained together, head and feet bare, clad only in their shirts. Soldiers, pot-bellied with ale, faces unshaven, but cruel with their sharp daggers, lances and swords. They were playing with a whore, a young girl, found guilty three times of soliciting within the city limits. She had been taken down to the pillory to be marked, branded on the face. I told the soldiers to leave her alone but they spat at me and beat her harder, I sometimes envy you the pure silence and peace of the monastery.

Inside the enclosure of the royal palace I kept well away from the main buildings and made my way to the outhouses, long one-storied buildings which house the royal records. Another argument with bumptious, self-important clerks but, at last, I got a list of pensioners; those men who had served Henry the Sixth and been rewarded for their office by being provided with a place at some monastery during their old age. I found one person, a junior secretarious to Henry the Sixth, Lawrence Callot. I called a clerk over and demanded to know where he was. More mumblings and objections, threats and knowing glances but at length I was told.

'Saint Bartholomew's Hospital, across Smithfield,' the clerk announced pompously. He smirked before adding, 'If he is still alive.'

I pulled out the scrap of parchment the Prior had given me at Chertsey. After more bullying, I discovered that the members of the Calais garrison which had accompanied the late King's body to Chertsey were usually garrisoned in the Tower.

'They are mercenaries, you see,' the clerk said. 'The King keeps them here in Westminster or the Tower.'

I nodded my thanks but the fellow had already turned his back. I went into

Smithfield, cutting my way through the bustling crowds until I came to the great open fields past the huge blackened stump where they burn heretics. Thank God, it was deserted except for a mangy old bear its owner had chained there whilst he had gone off to sup in some tavern. Near the great door of Saint Bartholomew's a swarthy stranger from behind the Gates of Hercules stood telling stories, his great cloak spread out before him.

'I sell dreams!' he shouted in a throaty voice. 'Come! Listen to my dreams!'

I ignored him. A madman, clothed in scarlet, a tame raven on each shoulder, ran up and screamed at me. I took no notice, walked by him and stopped a lay brother. He reminded me of you with his peaceful face and calm eyes, a soothing remedy for the violence and bounding ambition of the city. I mentioned Callot's name and he nodded.

'Oh, yes, he is here.'

'Is he sick?'

'Oh, yes,' he replied.

'Of what?'

'Of life!'

The brother smiled.

'He wants to die. Come!'

We went up some steps to the entrance of a great hall where crippled beggars sat sunning themselves, chatting, laughing, rolling a dice which they hid as the monk padded by. Inside, the long room was cool, sweet-smelling. Fresh rushes, sprinkled with crushed herbs, lay on the floor. The room was full of beds, two long rows, each separated from the other by white canvas sheets which hung on poles jutting out from the wall. The lay brother took me down the hall and stopped at one.

'Master Callot!' he called out. I looked at the figure on the bed, a veritable death's-head, propped up against the spittle-covered bolster. A thin face, a huge domed head, bald with tufts of hair, though above the slack mouth and sunken cheeks the eyes were bright and alert like those of an inquisitive bird. The lay brother sat down on a stool.

'You have a visitor, Lawrence.'

The old man cackled in reply.

'Then it must be someone from beyond the grave for everyone I know is dead!'

The lay brother smiled, rose and gestured for me to sit down whilst he softly walked away. I took his place on the stool while the old man, twisting his head, scrutinised me carefully.

'Master Callot,' I began. 'You were a secretarious to the late-lamented King, Henry the Sixth?'

The old man's eyes narrowed, he nodded his head.

'I am here,' I continued, 'not to upset you but to ask you questions, simple ones.'

Callot's eyes moved away. He smiled to himself as he stared at a point above my head.

'Oh, ask them then.'

'Tell me what you know of the King Henry.'

The slack lips smiled and tightened.

'Forsooth! Forsooth! The good Jesus have mercy!' He looked at me. 'King Henry was always saying that. He was no fool you know. He was tall, slender of body, thin-faced and deep-eyed. A clever scholar. Talk to those at Eton College or King's College, Cambridge. He founded both you know, yet they said he was a fool. Pshaw!' The old man stirred. 'He read more books than all of Oxford put together! You see,' he continued, 'he was a kind and gentle king. He didn't want the war in France. He used to pardon people; just before they were turned off the scaffold, Henry would send a messenger down, sometimes me. Always merciful, always compassionate. A good man but a bad king. Gentle as a dove he was, soft and kind. Do you know what he did?' He stopped to cough, clearing his chest and throat of the phlegm. I shook my head and smiled. 'If someone begged for alms, a favour, he would always say yes.'

I saw the old eyes fill with tears.

'So why did they call him a fool?' I asked.

'Two men,' Callot murmured in reply. 'The King was two men. His bitch of a wife saw to that.'

'What do you mean?'

'His bitch of a wife, the She-Wolf of Anjou,' the old man stirred and dragged himself closer. 'I'll tell you my confession,' he whispered hoarsely. 'King Henry was sane, saner than you or I. He married Margaret, eight years they were married. Henry was a man, a true Christian. Ignore the stories that he was monkish. He had a cock as firm and hard as you or I. But the Lady Margaret,' he coughed, turned and spat into a nearby bucket. 'Perhaps it was her fault. But for eight years his seed took no root. Then,' he squinted up at the ceiling, 'in 1453, aye, I remember, the winter, a cold, hard January when the Thames froze from bank to bank, the Queen told Henry that she was pregnant.' He stopped and fell back against the bolster, breathing hard. 'Henry was beside himself with glee,' Callot continued in a whisper. 'Proud he was. Every time I met him he boasted of it. Like some silly young boy who had taken his first maiden. I was so pleased for him.' He paused, lost in his own reverie. 'Then one day I found him in his own chamber, already mid-morning. Henry was still dressed in his night robes, his face unshaven, quiet, all life gone from his eyes. They said he had gone mad, succumbed to the same sickness of his French grandfather, Charles the Sixth. They always say that. They forget his own mother, Katherine of Valois, suffered no such sickness, whilst his father, the great conqueror, Henry the Fifth, was sane except for his lust for power.'

'But what happened?' I asked.

'King Henry told me later,' the old man continued in a matter-of-fact voice. 'He used to regain his wits at certain times. Margaret's chief adviser and leading general, Edward Beaufort, Duke of Somerset, was the Queen's lover. The child she carried was Somerset's. Somehow Henry found out. The King was not mad, the news simply drove his mind into the black pit of melancholy. After that, for the next eighteen years Henry lost the will to rule. He became nothing, a mere pawn, used by his wife,' the old man spat. 'Used by his bitch of a wife to defend the rights of her bastard son!'

Dear brother, I just sat there, transfixed by what I had heard. There had been stories, vulgar gossip, but here was King

Henry's own secretary openly confessing how Henry was no madman but simply driven mad by grief at his wife's infidelity. I sensed he spoke the truth. Henry the Sixth, gentle and kind, a great scholar, a patron of learning, a prince who adored his wife, cuckolded by one of his own courtiers. And what could he do? Trumpet the infidelity to the world to be made a laughing-stock both here and abroad? Or keep quiet and let the shock of such betrayal curdle his mind, tip his soul into the blackness of grief. I noticed how Callot's face had become flushed, I had kept him too long.

'Master Secretary,' I said.

He turned and smiled.

'No one has given me that title for years,' he said. 'When the great war broke out between Queen Margaret and the House of York, I left my post. That was twenty years ago.' He moved restlessly. 'What do you want?'

'One last question.'

He nodded.

'Do you think your master, the late King Henry, did he die in the Tower of this grief?' The old man laughed until his chest heaved and he broke into spasms of coughing.

'King Henry,' he replied breathlessly, 'King Henry was murdered! The prince was a saint. He fought against his melancholy and would never dream of taking his own life. When they took his body down to Saint Paul's and Black-friars, I went to view the corpse, just to say farewell. They had put him in a wooden casket, the body completely shrouded except for the face, exposed like that of a nun in her wimple. Do you know what I saw?'

I shook my head.

'Others witnessed it as well. I saw it bleed. Do you understand that? A victim of murder only bleeds in the presence of its perpetrators. I saw the blood behind the head. I saw it seep out through the cloths and stain the pillow. You are a doctor, you know what it means. Died in the Tower!' the old man cackled. 'King Henry, the Lord's anointed, that saint amongst princes. He was murdered! Murdered, I tell you!'

'They say Gloucester did it.' The old man added, 'Gloucester! He came into the Tower, stabbed him on King Edward's orders. How does it feel, physician, to work for regicides? Now, go!'

I left, bewildered by what he had told me. I did not even bother to thank the lay brother but walked as if in a dream out of St. Bartholomew's back across Smithfield and into the welcoming darkness of a tavern. I ordered the best of wines, sat and drank it in a few gulps, then had my cup refilled. What was I involved in? What am I doing in this, Stephen? I could have wept for the waste of time and bitterly wondered — Is this what our father died for? For hypocrites and regicides? Like others, I had accepted the story of how Henry the Sixth was a fool, a witless numbskull but I knew this was a lie. A King who could found colleges at Eton and Cambridge and study books. What fool? And his death?

I thought of my colleagues on this commission: Trollope, the lawyer; Gough, the professional killer; Rokesley, the adroit courtier, and those they served. Edward, the so-called 'golden boy', a man who had fought Henry's wife to the finish. George of Clarence, treacherous, ever ready to change sides, as fickle as ever he was. Finally, Richard of Gloucester, small, tense, wiry, a prince steeped in blood or so they said. I feel this commission is part of a greater game, that I am walking down paths and do not know where they lead.

I finished my drink and went to see an old patient, a man well past his eighty-fifth summer. He lives in Aldersgate in a street just opposite the convent of Greyfriars. A small, two-storied house, always clean though he lives by himself. A man possessed of all his faculties, despite his age. Nothing is more calming than to sit with him in his small enclosed herb garden, complete with one straggly apple tree and pass the time of day. I only know him as Benedict, a man hale and hearty in mind as he is in body. He, too, is a keen collector of ancient coins. He greeted me effusively and we spent an hour as the sun set whilst he showed me his collection of coins, dug from the empty mudflats along the Thames. A recent one fascinated me for it bore the head of Constantinus Chlorus, the father of Constantine, the first Christian Emperor. My conversation with him pushed back the shadows and, when I left, I felt refreshed enough to go into the Greyfriars church. I lit candles in the Lady Chapel and prayed for the souls of our parents. Like all men, my mind wandered, and I was about to leave when I heard the slither of leather behind me. I turned and walked into the centre of the nave.

'Who is there?' I called. No answer except the squeak of mice in the darkness. I turned and genuflected towards the altar and left, the hair on the nape of my neck curling like that of a dog. I was certain, and still am, that I was being followed and watched.

It was dark by the time I reached home. Blanche was waiting for me, sitting in the buttery, a piece of tapesty on her lap. Across the table sat Rokesley, cool, tactful, the born courtier, I could see he had been making her laugh. He rose as I entered.

'Luke, I have been waiting for you. Where have you been?'

'Walking the streets, I suppose,' Blanche pretended to snap, though her eyes danced with mischief. 'For God's sake, Simon,' she cried. 'Look at the way the man is dressed!'

I gazed down self-consciously at my blue robe.

'My wife spends my silver,' I bantered back. 'And does nothing but sit at home and entertain strange men!'

Blanche rose in mock anger, counting on her fingers to emphasise the tasks she had done. 'I have sewn, cleaned, drawn up accounts, been to the market and, as you say,' she grinned wickedly at Rokesley, 'entertained your strange friends.' She stooped under the table and brought out a bundle, it looked like an expensive bale of cloth. Then she shook it free, holding it up for both of us to see. 'A new gown,' she called, 'one fit for a royal physician.'

I looked at the robe. Blanche had

chosen well. My favourite colour. Dark blue, trimmed around the collar and cuffs with costly fur, voluminous sleeves, gold clasps and, practical as ever, the robe had deep pockets. Blanche made me try it on, clapping her hands with glee as she pronounced it a perfect fit. I supposed I caught her mood.

'Do you know why she bought me this, Rokesley?' I pretended to sneer. 'Not for me. Oh, no! She likes to use my old robes whenever she goes in the garden.'

Blanche pouted.

'You are only jealous of the time I spend in it!' she cried.

Rokesley stood and watched this banter. He smiled, though I could gather from his pursed lips that he was impatient to talk to me so I took him into my chamber off the hall. He asked me what progress I had made. I told him what he wanted, depicting Callot's statement more as the ravings of an old man than what I secretly regarded as the truth. Rokesley watched me closely and told me that, despite Ashby's death, the commission would meet again. I bade him adieu. I did not tell him of my fears. Only you know, Stephen. God save us, brother. Remember us in your prayers. September 1477.

Letter 3

Luke, physician, to Brother Stephen, monk at Aylesford Prior, health and greetings.

Blanche sends her love and good wishes. She has begun to press me on why we cannot visit you, though I have explained the rules of your order. The Carmelites are enclosed, visits are limited to one every few years and we have to wait. She says such rules are stupid, as are any made by men. I have told her the Carmelite order also has foundations for women and, if she is not careful, she may find herself in one. She just made faces at me and, taking my old robe, flounced out to her beloved garden. Nevertheless, my heart echoes her sentiments. Despite the years, Stephen, I still miss you.

As you know, these letters are taken by a friend of mine, Robert Tyndall, a draper's journeyman, he can be trusted and says he faithfully leaves my letters at the friary gate. This time I am asking him to take a present for you, a copy of Pope Gregory's 'Cura Pastoralis'. I know you cannot accept personal gifts but Robert will leave a message that it is my donation to your monastery's slender library.

I was ill for two days after I wrote to you last. God knows why. Some evil humour of the mind. I felt melancholic and withdrawn. I say this honestly, the King's commission darkens my soul and makes me frightened. You know I am not a timid man but, as I said, it does tax my health. I eagerly seized the opportunity to stay at home, examining my collection of ancient coins, trying to determine beneath the grime and the marks of centuries from which Imperial mint they came. At last, however, God be thanked, I was restored to my usual good spirits and went by wherry boat to the Tower. I know the boatman, Watkins, well.

You, too, have met him just before you went to Aylesford; a small, thin weasel of a man with a merry, stout wife and a host of children. He has the agility and strength of a monkey and constantly regales me with his sexual prowess. I quietly listen, trying to hide my grin and wondered what his secret was. If I knew I would put it in a physic and make a fortune selling it to court and the powerful London merchants. Watkins safely delivered me at the Tower wharf. Despite the sun, the fortress looked as grim as ever, heavily guarded, soldiers, on foot or mounted, constantly coming or going. I was admitted when I showed my warrants at the Lion Gate and went up between the huge walls onto the green around the White Keep. I was surprised to see Richard of Gloucester there with his group of henchmen around him, Tyrrell, Ratcliffe and others. He raised a gloved hand in greeting, tossing back his green, ermine-trimmed robe. I would have passed by but he beckoned me over.

'I trust you are well, physician?' The group around him stood silent and watchful. 'You are busy about my brother's matters?'

'Yes, Your Grace.'

'So, what brings you here?'

'This is the place King Henry died,' I

replied. 'You must remember it well, Your Grace. The twenty-first May, the eve of the Ascension.' God be my witness, Gloucester did not turn a hair but nodded and talked amiably about those stirring days. I studied his thin, cunning face and heavily lidded eyes.

'So,' he smiled. 'Is King Henry to be canonised?'

'I do not know, Your Grace. But I certainly will for the time and hardship this task has caused me!'

Duke Richard's face creased into a grin like that of some schoolboy caught in mischief. He clapped me on the shoulder and guided me away from his companions, leaning closer so I caught the wine fumes from his breath.

'You are a physician, Luke,' he whispered. 'Renowned for your wisdom. I give you warning. There is danger! Be prudent!' He smiled again, nodded and walked back to rejoin his companions. Now alarmed, I strode across the green, around the great keep to where the garrison had its quarters. A soldier sat on the grass, cleaning his hauberk with an old rag and a small pot of dry sand. He looked up as I approached.

'Pancius Cantrone?' I asked.

'What about him?'

'I would like to speak to him.'

'What business is that of mine?'

I clinked my purse and drew out two pennies. The man grinned and, turning his head, spat.

'Of course, I can help,' he smiled. He pointed towards an outbuilding. 'You should find him over there, sleeping, drinking, wining or farting, whatever we do whenever we are not soldiering. Tell them Osbert sent you.'

I tossed the two coins down and walked away.

At the guard house I went through the same ritual. More coins exchanged hands and I finally learnt that Cantrone was on guard duty high on the northern wall. I went up the steep steps, not caring to look down as the wind buffeted and shook me. The parapet walk was narrow, moss-strewn and I walked slowly along, keeping my left hand on the crenellated wall. Beneath me stretched the mudflats, interspersed with old ruins, the remains of buildings which housed Caesar's legions. I saw the white flash of a gull as it whined and keened, looking for food. The winds, the high wall and the lonely call of the birds made me feel strange as if walking in a dream. I saw a soldier crouched against the battlements, huddled in his cloak, his back to the wind. He stirred as I approached.

'Pancius Cantrone!' I called out. The man stood upright. I could not distinguish his features because of the heavy conical helmet and broad noseguard. 'Pancius Cantrone!' I repeated. The man nodded, gesturing and took off his helmet to reveal an olive-skinned face, deep dark eyes and a small goatee beard which fringed a mouth of broken teeth. When he smiled it was like some dog baring his fangs.

'Pancius Cantrone,' I began. 'I have some questions for you.' The smile faded.

'What do you want?'

I shifted my belt so he heard my purse clink, yet I had my suspicions. If he had given the sheath and cap to the monks of

Chertsey then he was a brave man with some sense of virtue and, perhaps, could not be bought. He leaned exasperatedly against the wall, the spear resting in the fold of his arm.

'I am Cantrone,' he replied in a guttural voice. 'So what is your business?'

'You are English?'

'My mother was, my father Genoese.'

'You have always been a soldier?' I asked.

He shrugged.

'To beg, I am unable,' he said with a smile, quoting from the gospel. I noticed his face was crooked, the nose slightly bent, one eye lower than the other.

'You are a professional soldier? A member of the Calais garrison? You were in the funeral cortege of Henry the Sixth?' Cantrone's eyes narrowed. 'You were,' I said hurriedly. 'You also took the cap and sheath to Chertsey Abbey?'

His face paled. 'You did, didn't you?' I pleaded. 'Please I mean no harm or evil to you. You have my word, I will swear it.' I tapped my purse so he could hear the chink of coins. 'You could be richer than you have ever been if you tell me the truth.'

Cantrone looked out over the wall. At last he sighed and stood straight, cocking his head to squint up at the sky.

'I have about one hour of duty left. I will talk, but not here. Be in the guard room when I come down. You have my word. I will meet you there.'

I was glad to be off the parapet walk and spent the time pacing round the Tower looking at the new bombardes, culverins and siege machines the King's crafsmen were building. The royal menagerie had two lions, rather old and sleepy and they did not even bother to move when I looked into their pit. By the time I returned to the guard room Cantrone was there, a loaf in one hand a pannikin of wine in the other. He led me out onto the grass, offering me both bread and wine but I refused. He squatted on the ground and bit off huge chunks, swilling them down with mouthfuls of wine, pronouncing himself satisfied with a loud, noisy belch.

'Your questions?' he squinted at me.

'But, first, who are you?'

'My name is Luke Chichele. I am a physician. I am here on the King's orders to ask questions about the late King Henry the Sixth. I have warrants if you wish to see them.'

Cantrone turned and hawked.

'A waste of time,' he replied. 'I cannot read. So, ask your questions.'

'You were on guard duty,' I said, 'in the Tower when Henry died?'

'Yes, I was,' he agreed. 'I and other members of the garrison. We are professional soldiers. The only ones King Edward could really trust. You may remember the events of 1471. Henry was in London and in the early spring Edward had to face two armies. One in the north led by Margaret's general, that great bastard, the Earl of Warwick. The second, an invasion force under the great bitch, Queen Margaret herself and her son, Prince Edward. Henry, the old King, had been Edward's prisoner for years. He was kept quite comfortable here.' Cantrone pointed to one of the great round donjons, 'The Wakefield Tower. I will show it to you later.'

'Was Henry kept close?' I asked.

'Whilst Edward was king,' Cantrone answered, 'Henry was allowed to wander round the Tower. You may remember he was out of our custody for a short while. Clarence went over to the Lancastrians. He and their general, Warwick, staged a sudden coup. Henry was taken from the Tower and paraded through London, but Edward the Fourth and Gloucester returned to England and Henry was recaptured.' Cantrone paused and took a fresh swig of wine. 'Indeed, it was pathetic. Henry seemed more pleased to see Edward the Fourth than he did his own wife's generals.' Cantrone stopped and squinted up at the sun. 'Now, what did he say when Edward met him? Ah, yes, that's it — 'Cousin of York, you are very welcome. I hold my life to be in no danger in your hands'.'

'He said that?'

'Oh, yes,' Cantrone replied, 'and in his turn Edward told him not to worry about anything. You know what happened then? Edward marched north to defeat the Lancastrians; his brother Clarence rejoined him and Edward smashed Warwick just north of London at a place called Barnet, that was on Easter Sunday. On the same day Queen Margaret, her son and Somerset landed in the west country, Edward hurried off to meet them. Again he was victorious. Somerset and the rest were killed, including the young prince, and the Yorkists marched back to London.'

'What happened to Henry?' I interrupted.

Cantrone shrugged.

'Oh, everything here was confusing. Nobody knew what would happen. While Edward was in the west, a Lancastrian general called the Bastard of Fauconberg, attacked London. King Edward's queen and the rest of the family took refuge here. The place was as busy as a beehive.'

'And Henry?'

'He was confined to his own quarters. Very few people saw him.'

'Anyone in particular?'

'Yes, the Queen visited him once.'

'You mean Elizabeth Woodville?'

'Yes. Yes, she went across but the meeting was amicable enough.'

'Anyone else?'

'Two other men. One a priest, John Ashby, Clarence's chaplain. He came often, especially in the last few days, and the other person was a lawyer, a funny name, Trollope.'

Cantrone wiped his mouth on the back of his hand. 'Yes, that's his name, Trollope. I remember that very clearly because the Constable of the Tower, the same man now, Sir John Audley, he wrote special passes for them and we had to remember their names. Perhaps you should ask him.'

'And the last day?' I asked. 'The day King Henry died?'

Cantrone made a grimace with his mouth.

'I remember it was a Wednesday, the day before the Feast of the Ascension. King Edward re-entered London late in the afternoon. He went to Westminster, then he and his two brothers came here. There was a great deal of rejoicing, singing and shouting. I saw Queen

Margaret, Henry's wife, she had been brought back into London sitting in a cart. Our captain told us the danger was past. The Tower gates were thrown open, people were coming and going.' He stopped and chewed his lip.

'So when did Henry die?'

Cantrone sighed.

'I don't know. We were roused from our quarters well after the third watch, past midnight. I and four others. The captain took us across to the Wakefield Tower. Come!'

We got up and walked across the grass to the great round donjon Cantrone had pointed out. We entered a small postern door and up a damp, stone, spiral staircase through another door and we were into a spacious, round chamber. The walls were bare except for a wooden crucifix. The furniture consisted of a bed on trestles, a small cupboard, a battered leather chest and two stools, one with a leg broken. The place was uninhabited, the floor still covered with dirty rushes.

'King Henry lived here,' Cantrone began. 'Sometimes he was allowed out into the garden. However, when we were brought across that night,' he pointed over to the bed, 'King Henry was lying there, his body had already been prepared for burial.'

He shivered. 'He looked like a ghost shrouded in white. Yet his face looked peaceful, the eyes closed as if asleep.'

'Did you see any blood?'

'No, the shroud round his head was very thick.'

'And the dagger-sheath?'

'Oh, I found that later. After we took the body down to Blackfriars. The captain told me to clean the chamber and I found it amongst the rushes, half buried.'

'Were there any blood-stains?'

'A little, on the rushes.'

'Who else was in the chamber?' I asked.

Cantrone bit his lip.

'Richard of Gloucester. He was just sitting on a stool beside the corpse. His face was very pale. He was dressed in half-armour. I thought he had been drinking though he gave us our orders clearly enough.'

'And the sheath? Why did you give it to

Chertsey Abbey?'

Cantrone turned towards me and spread his hands.

'I don't know why. I knew if I handed it in, questions might be asked and I was frightened. If the sheath was found on me, I could expect further trouble.' He looked at me beseechingly. 'I suppose I panicked.' He licked his lips nervously. 'Look, physician, we all know Henry was murdered. I am a soldier, I take my chances. Moreover, I liked King Henry, he was kind, pious. So, when we arrived at Chertsey, I handed the sheath over.'

'Did you recognise it?'

'No, that's what made me all the more frightened. It was just a common sheath. There are many like it in the Tower armoury.'

'And the dagger?'

Pancius shook his head.

'I don't know.' He looked away.

Cantrone was lying but the stubborn, withdrawn look in his dark eyes meant any further questions would only estrange him further. I dug into my purse and drew out a gold coin.

'Pancius,' I said quietly. 'I am sure you are innocent of the King's blood. You have been very helpful.'

He took the money.

'One last question?' I said. 'You soldiers talk amongst each other. Whom do you think killed King Henry?'

Cantrone shrugged.

'They say Gloucester.'

'Anything else?'

'No, that's all I remember.'

I patted him on the arm.

'Then, sir, I bid you adieu.'

I turned and went down the stairs but Cantrone called after me.

'One final matter, Master!'

I looked back at him.

'What is it?'

'King Henry never spoke much but I heard a story. One day, I forget whom, someone baited him about whether Prince Edward, his son, was truly his or of bastard issue. King Henry replied that only God knew the truth, as He did about the House of York. Is that not strange?'

'Yes, yes,' I said.

I thanked him and walked across to the

royal apartments. I stopped a guard and asked to see Sir John Audley, Constable of the Tower. After a little bullying and a small amount of bribery, I was allowed into the royal apartments and told to wait in a small chamber off the great hall. I must have spent an hour biding my time, watching the sun set through the narrow slit window. At last Audley arrived, a typical soldier, abrupt, bluff, hair closely cropped. He looked as if he was in a constant state of war. I explained my commission but, making no reference to Cantrone, asked him what happened the night King Henry died. He raised his eyebrows and shrugged, King Henry's death meant little to him.

'King Edward,' he began abruptly, 'arrived in London from the west country. Eventually he, his brothers and all their retinue were here. Queen Elizabeth was sheltering in the royal apartments. King Edward came to meet his wife. You know procedures. Once the King is here, my office lapses.'

'But surely,' I insisted. 'There was a guard on King Henry's quarters?'

'Why should there be!' Audley snapped back. 'The crisis was over. The Lancastrian generals dead, Margaret of Anjou a prisoner, her own son tossed into a common grave at Tewkesbury, whilst King Henry was too simple to find his way out of a room, never mind rule a kingdom! People were coming and going. The first I knew of it was that Henry was dead.'

'Murdered?' I asked.

Audley smirked.

'Murder? The legitimate king was, and still is, Edward the fourth. If he gave an order for Henry to be executed, I would have accepted it. Who cares if a madman dies?'

'Do you think he was executed?' I asked.

'No, I don't. I believe he killed himself.'

'How so?'

'It's been done before,' Audley replied. 'Henry had been a prisoner for years. He receives news that his wife is captured, his son dead, so he dashes his head against a wall.' He must have glimpsed the disbelief in my eyes. 'You may not think so but I have seen it done, here, in this very building.'

I could see Audley would be of little use. I thanked him, went out into the darkness and made my way home. The curfew imposed during the pestilence had now been lifted and the streets were still busy. I felt disturbed, alarmed by my visit to the Tower. What had Gloucester meant when he told me to be careful? Why had Ashby and Trollope visited the imprisoned king? What did King Henry mean by God knowing the truth about the House of York? Why hadn't Ashby and Trollope explained themselves? Was Audley right? Did Henry commit suicide or did Gloucester kill him? And where had the dagger gone? Who had wielded it? And why had they been so careless in leaving the sheath in the death chamber?

I tell you this, Stephen, these questions vexed my mind and kept me busy for days after. I could see no solution and was almost grateful when Rokesley sent me a letter inviting me, and me alone, to a banquet at Westminster, after which I and others would meet Renaldi, the papal legate. Blanche objected at not being invited and turned away when I tried to explain how I had no choice in the matter. When I arrived at Westminster and saw the splendid preparations, I could understand her disappointment. The banqueting hall was a blaze of light, with candles fixed on huge wheels, hoisted high above the room. There must have been hundreds, tall and white, they hung like fire-flies. The walls were covered with tapestries of every conceivable hue, the best the royal wardrobes could supply. The tablets were covered in snow-white cloths and napkins and each servant was clad in blue and gold livery, bearing the sun of York. They served us course after course; venison, boar's head, goose, swan, heron in clover, all stuffed with herbs and served in rich sauces; sweet pastries, bowls of cream, pastries and jellies shaped in castles, griffins, dragons and other strange beasts. The galley was packed with musicians. On the dais, the royal table, under a canopy of cloth of gold, was dazzling to the eye. The King, his Queen, Gloucester and

Clarence, all dressed in blue and silver; the place of eminence being given to Renaldi, the papal legate. He seemed bemused as any of us by Edward's lavish hospitality.

Bearing in mind my own advice to my patients in these pestilential times, I ate little but the fruit, and I was only too pleased when the King rose as a sign that the banquet was over.

Once the festivities were finished and the guests departing, Rokesley appeared as if from nowhere, touching me gently on the elbow, whispering I was to follow him. In a small room, perhaps a robing chamber behind the great dais, I found the rest of the commission waiting. Renaldi, a little inebriated; Gough as dour as ever but vigilant and watchful as a cat; Trollope was in an expansive mood, face flushed, eyes excited as he still cradled a huge goblet of wine. I watched carefully for I wanted words with him. Finally, Rokesley, who must have been at the banquet but, like me, appeared not to have touched either food or drink. He began the meeting, drawing reports from each of us whilst Renaldi sat at the top of the table, eyes half closed. I had to smile to myself. The King had been most cunning. First, he had lavished his hospitality on Renaldi, dazzling him with the splendour of his court. Now Renaldi was to hear from those who had been investigating the reign of the man whose crown Edward had usurped. Nevertheless, Renaldi was no fool, and he became more alert as the meeting progressed. I lied and so, I am sure, did all the rest. Trollope described the ineptitude of Henry's administration, the collapse of markets at home and abroad, the sheer fecklessness of the King. Gough described the bloody civil war, one futile battle after another, cleverly catalogued to depict Henry's reign as one deserted by Heaven. I also spoke but, God forgive me, I did not tell the truth but said there was little cause to regard Henry as a saint. I quoted Audley, the Constable of the Tower, hinted how Henry may have taken his own life. As I have remarked, Renaldi was no man's fool. He must have sensed that we were all hiding something, deliberately concealing the truth or only allowing those facts to be aired which would fit our case.

I thought of you, Stephen. If I described your life, hidden in a monastery, many men would regard it as a waste. If I described the life of St. Francis and only concentrated on certain aspects then the saint of Assisi could easily be seen as a fool. I also thought of St. Paul's words about the Christian faith being something the angels would wonder at and a spectacle for other men to laugh at. Henry the Sixth's life accorded with all of this and perhaps Renaldi sensed the truth. He may have been full of food and good wine and the King might have expected him to call the matter to an end. However, when Renaldi had heard us all out, he leaned over the table, steepling his dark, slender fingers.

'I think, gentlemen,' he said in his perfect English. 'you have given me some information but not enough for the Holy Father to dismiss this case out of hand. You hold the King's commission. I hold mine from the Pope. I must ask you to

105

continue with your task.' He sensed our disappointment. God knows, we all had our reasons for wanting this matter over and done with but, like born courtiers, we smiled and bowed, hid our true feelings and promised to continue.

Once the meeting ended, I avoided Rokesley and watched Trollope out of the corner of my eyes. When he slipped like some rat out of the door, I followed swiftly, allowing him to walk ahead of me until he was free of the palace buildings. I ran up to him, catching him by the arm.

'Master Trollope,' I said. 'I wish words with you.' Like any lawyer, he looked arrogantly back.

'What is it, Doctor?' he asked sarcastically. 'Well, ask it, man!'

'Why didn't you tell the commission you visited the late King Henry in the Tower?'

'Oh, but I did, I told Rokesley.'

'Well, then,' I replied, 'we share the same commission so tell me.'

'It's none of your business!' Trollope snapped.

'Oh, Master Lawyer, it is. May I

remind you how I am supposed to enquire into the direct causes of Henry's death.'

'My visits to the late King Henry had nothing to do with that.'

I stepped back and folded my arms beneath my robe, thinking briefly how pleased I was Blanche had bought it for the evening had turned cold.

'If you do not tell me,' I replied smoothly, 'I shall resign my commission. Tell Rokesley, perhaps the Queen, even the King himself.'

I do not know which of my barbs went home but I saw the fear blossom in his drunken face.

'Look,' Trollope said with a sigh. 'My visit to the late King Henry had nothing to do with the commission. Now I work in the Inns of Court but years earlier I was an attorney.'

'Who for?'

'His Grace, George Duke of Clarence. I was a member of his household.' He took a deep breath. 'You may remember Clarence's loyalties were not always with his brother. During the last months of the war when Henry was in the Tower, I acted as an intermediary.' He peered closer. 'Don't look so shocked, Master Physician, there are many at court who once fought for the House of Lancaster or were associated with it. Even the Queen's kin once had loyalties other than York.'

'Well,' I replied, regretting the words as soon as they were out of my mouth, 'Clarence must have had a great deal to say to King Henry. After all, you were not the only intermediary. Our former priestly colleague, John Ashby, had also occasion to visit King Henry in prison.'

Now Trollope stepped back, his lips curling like a dog snarling.

'Whatever you are hinting at, either speak,' he leaned closer. 'Or,' he hissed, 'keep your mouth shut! I, too, have influence, I am the King's serjeant-at-law. Look to your potions, Physician, and try not to trap me.'

The fellow immediately spun on his heel and walked out into the darkness. I watched him go and made my own way home to Blanche and her constant questions about the banquet, the scene, the food, the wine, the colour and texture of the Queen's gown, how did she look and to whom I had talked. I replied with a mixture of truth and lies and hid my own anxiety. Never once telling her how this business vexed me or my suspicions of being followed. I peered through the window and my fears grew as I saw the watchers in the shadows slip deeper into the darkness.

Late the next morning I decided to return to Chertsey but this time by myself in a more business-like fashion. I apologised to Blanche but explained that the matter was pressing. I was about to leave and was in the buttery supervising one of the maids preparing a pot of ale and some strips of cooked meat, when I heard a thundering at the door. Blanche ran in, her face white, her eyes staring. My heart lurched with fear. Had something gone wrong? Blanche, speechless, stuttered.

'It is the Duke! Luke, he's here! He's here!' At first, I thought she meant Gloucester, but then Clarence pushed his way through the door, two of his retainers in close attendance. The Duke's face was still flushed from a hard night's drinking, though his eyes were sharp and alert. He was dressed in brown and green fustian with a short woollen cloak thrown around his shoulders. I could tell from the leather gauntlets and the long Spanish riding boots that the Duke intended a day's hunting. Outside in the passageways one of his servitors carried a hawk. I heard the bells of the jesse as it moved on the man's wrist, and the soft soothing noises made to keep the bird calm. Clarence stopped, openly admiring Blanche, before giving me the most sardonic of bows.

'Master Physician,' he said merrily, 'I thought we should personally call on you.'

'Is His Grace ill?' I asked.

Clarence grinned.

'No, not ill, though I have news of a possible fatal illness.' He looked around, gesturing with his hand for his companions to leave. 'But for your ears alone, Physician.' He bowed at Blanche. 'Be not afraid, my lady, my men will take good care of you.'

'Blanche,' I interrupted. 'There is no need to stay. You have work in the garden.'

'I have work in this house!' she snapped, glaring at the Duke. 'And I will decide where I go and what I do!' and, picking my old cloak up from the bench, she swung it round her shoulders and stormed through the open door into the garden. Clarence watched her go before smiling and closing the door behind her. He then spun round dramatically and leaned his back against it.

'Physician, you are working on the commission?' I nodded. The Duke seemed to lose his mask of merriment, chewing at his lip, he crossed his arms and stared at me as if trying to decide something.

'Ashby,' he continued slowly, 'was also working on this matter but now he is dead. Murdered they say.'

'So men say,' I agreed.

The Duke shook his head.

'And now you question Trollope?'

'You have no objection, Your Grace?'

'Oh, I have no objection at all,

Physician, but I do have a warning for you and the same to Trollope. Whoever killed Ashby may want to kill you.' He came closer. 'Nothing,' he whispered, 'nothing is what it seems to be.'

'I thank you for your warning, Your Grace. But surely you have not come here just to tell me that. I suspect you have asked Trollope the same thing.'

The Duke smiled.

'And what would that be?'

'Did Ashby tell us something? Something, my Lord, you would like to know?'

Clarence threw his head back, giggling like a young girl. I gazed at the light blue eyes and shivered. I had heard rumours. Men say that Clarence himself is not sane.

'My Lord,' I hurried on, 'Ashby told me nothing, though what he might have said,' I broke off. 'God knows.'

Clarence took one of his leather gauntlets and came over, waving it in my face.

'Physician, you are a shrewd man. Walk carefully.'

'Strange,' I replied, resenting his

overbearing attitude. 'Your brother, my Lord of Gloucester, gave me the same warning.'

'My Lord of Gloucester,' Clarence mimicked in reply, 'could well be advised to take some of the medicine and advice he metes out to others.'

After saying this Clarence brushed by me and swept out of the house, leaving the door open and calling for his servants to follow. I heard him and his party mount and the sound of their horses' hoof beats fade into the distance. I went out into the garden and, doing what I could, calmed Blanche. I called my two apprentices and the maids, instructing them to take good care of their mistress and to unbar the door to no one but myself.

The journey to Chertsey was uneventful enough. I hired a boat, thankfully it was not rowed by Watkins with his litany of sexual exploits so I could sit in silence and wonder what Clarence had meant. Ashby's death is, I believe, crucial. That priest knew something, some information so dreadful it had cost him his life. His murderer now wondered whether we were party to it. Clarence had come to find that out, prompted to do so by my interrogation of Trollope the previous evening. Yet, like his brother Richard, Clarence had taken steps to warn me about what? The death of a forlorn king? Or was there something else? Something Henry knew and had told Ashby? Was Clarence or Gloucester (or both) the murderer?

Such thoughts still puzzled me as I walked up the gravel strewn path to Chertsey Abbey. This time I was more fortunate, although I was taken to the Prior, he seemed eager enough to pass me on to his abbot who had returned from his travels. The latter was a true monk and looked it. The tonsure perfectly cut, the brown robe of poor quality over his thin body and his emaciated face dominated by large, dark eyes which seemed to probe my very soul.

I found I could not lie and told him truthfully the problem. His abbey was the last resting-place of Henry the Sixth, the late but little lamented King of England.

Some men, I commented, had considered Henry a fool but a few regarded him as a saint. The abbot heard me out.

'Come, follow me!' he ordered abruptly.

He rose from behind his great wooden desk and took me round the cloister into the abbey library, a dark musty place, smelling of ink, scrubbed parchment and costly leather. On either side were the carrels for the monks to study, each had shelves with great tomes chained and padlocked to them. The abbot led me through them into a smaller chamber containing a huge chest, closed and sealed with five locks. He took a heavy bunch of keys from under his robe and carefully unlocked each of the clasps, pushed back the creaking lid and pulled out a small, white roll of parchment which he held out to me.

'Read this,' he said. 'You can sit here. I will lock you in the chamber for you cannot take this manuscript away. But read it carefully and then make your judgment about King Henry.' He slipped quietly out of the room. I heard him lock the door and I squatted down in a corner, undoing the red cord, and began to study the manuscript. At first, I grinned but the list grew longer; a catalogue of miracles, worked at Henry's tomb, not just anecdotes but, as a lawyer would say, chapter and verse: the name, the date, the place. A few were pathetic stories but others caught my interest as a doctor. A man who had suffered from the falling sickness cured after visting the royal tomb. A child who had drowned, spitting out the water after some priest had intoned a prayer to King Henry: a man hanged for some crime he did not commit, left swinging for hours on the gallows but, when cut down, he revived and walked away. A woman, riddled with leprosy, another with internal bleeding, all the revolting, macabre illnesses which would have made any doctor despair. All gone, cured sometimes in the twinkling of an eye.

I admit I could explain away a few of these cases and I am sceptical of miracles. The human soul has unplumbed depths and who can challenge the power of the mind? I have heard of men in the east who can lie on swords unscathed, walk through furnaces unharmed, levitate their bodies from the ground. Yet I am no cynic and the record of miracles would have disturbed even the most hardened mind. I read through the list again. The abbot had been most careful, each claim being thoroughly investigated. I sat in that small, dusty room and shivered. My suspicions began to harden. The Yorkist warlords had killed a saint and, like the Gadarene swine, we had all followed, making the dreadful error that because Henry was not a good king he could not have possibly been a great saint. I thought of Henry's desolate tomb and, in a way, could understand him. What use of power, the glory and the banners? It could all be a moment's sadness. As the psalmist said 'Under the sun nothing lasts'. Had Henry understood that? What profit from Kingship when your own wife had betrayed you?

The abbot returned almost an hour later, unlocking the door and slipping into the room. He took the roll of parchment from my hand.

'You have read it, Physician?'

'I have,' I replied. 'I do not know what to say. I deal with disease and possible cures. The Church teaches that miracles are acts of faith, the result of God's intervention. All I can say, as a doctor, is that the manuscript gives serious cause to reflect on who King Henry the Sixth of England really was.'

The abbot just looked at me.

'If we do that,' I continued, 'we must then consider the possibility that sanctity is a form of madness.'

The abbot smiled.

'I believe Henry was a saint,' he answered. He crouched down beside my stool. 'He may have been more,' and drew out from beneath his gown a small, narrow casket. He undid the clasps and lifted the lid. There, on a satin lining, lay a long, cruel dagger. Nothing extraordinary about it. Scores like it could be found in the tower stores or strapped to the belt of any man-at-arms. The abbot lifted the dagger out and gave it to me.

'The soldiers who brought the King's

corpse down here,' he said. 'One of them, a swarthy character, also brought this. He said he had found it in the King's death cell. He was frightened and did not know what to do with it. If he surrendered it, someone might realise that the soldier knew the truth. They may even have accused him of being a perpetrator of the crime.'

'The crime being the death of Henry?' I asked.

'Yes,' the abbot replied.

'Was the dagger stained?'

The abbot pursed his lips.

'Strange,' he murmured, 'you should say that. There was blood, but not on the blade.' He pointed down. 'Here, on the dagger hilt. In between the metal coils around the handle, small spots of blood and strands of grey hair which matched that of the dead King.' He looked full at me. 'I believe King Henry is both a saint and a martyr. He died a violent death. That's why his body bled when it lay at Blackfriars and Saint Paul's. You know a corpse never bleeds?'

'Except,' I interrupted, 'in the presence

of its murderers!'

'Exactly,' the abbot replied. He rose, raising me up by the hand.

'I do not know whether you are a good man, Physician, but in this matter I sense a terrible danger. What I have shown you is for your eyes only but there are many who believe, as I do, that Henry was a saint. Not only the names found in the manuscript go to Lincoln or York. You will find the late King Henry venerated as a holy man. In some churches they even revere him through paintings or statues. Don't you realise, Luke, any one who could slay a man like Henry, would think nothing of killing someone like you?'

I left the abbey, the monk's dire warning ringing in my ears. Henry the Sixth had been murdered, brutally so. I shivered. I was possibly working with his murderers, the very assassins who had stabbed out his life. I had no illusions about who had given the dagger to Chertsey Abbey. Cantrone had not told me everything and I told the waiting boatman to take me up to the Tower quay and wait. I found the entrance to the fort

120

heavily guarded; red flaring sulphur torches on either side of the portcullis and long columns of dusty men-at-arms crossing the mudflats towards one of the Tower's postern gates. My unease grew. Something was wrong. The guards at the entrance gate had been doubled and over the captain's shoulder I could see mailed forces milling about in the courtyard. I asked the officer if I could see Cantrone. He looked at me strangely and thrust my warrant back into my hand.

'Cantrone is not here,' he replied.

I pressed him further but his hand slipped on to the hilt of his sword, so I shrugged and went back to the boat.

I was tired when I landed at Westminster Steps, locked in my own thoughts. My life would have gone without me even thinking as the assassin struck suddenly from the shadows, cloaked and hooded, all I saw was the glint of the raised knife. I dodged sideways and perhaps my sudden movement surprised my assailant. He slipped on the cobbles and fell with a winding crash to the ground, the knife skittering out of his hand. I am no fighter.

I did not pause even for a second glance but gathered my cloak around me and ran like the wind; slipping and cursing. I took short cuts down alleyways and narrow, darkened streets, until I arrived breathless at my own house. There I rested for a while to calm my breathing, and knocked at the door, hiding my fears behind a mask of good-humoured tiredness. Sweet God, I hoped Blanche would not sense my fears. She chatted on about the herbs she had been crushing from her garden; fennel, mint, thyme. I was relieved to shelter in the darkness of my own bed and try to reason away my fears. Pray for me, as I do for you, Stephen.

Written 24th September 1477.

Letter 4

Luke Chichele, physician, to his brother Stephen, monk of Aylesford Priory, all health and greetings.

Almost a month since I wrote to you last, Stephen, and nothing has occurred to allay my fears. A week after my return from Chertsey I interrogated others who knew the late King. Minor officials, clerks, servitors and retainers. All were evasive. Everything they said was shadowy, with little substance, yet I saw the truth in their faces, each one bearing witness to the late King's charity and his piety. Oh, yes, as a King, he was feckless. Henry could not rule because he did not want to rule. Never have I heard of such a man more suited for the monastery than the court or field of battle.

I hid my fears from Blanche and I tried not to move far from home. Rokesley had sent me a letter enquiring what progress I had made but I ignored him. Elizabeth, the Queen, also sent a letter. A short, sweet note saying how she and her children missed me. I was to return to court as soon as possible and how she nagged the King daily to release me from my duties. He, however, had declined, replying that until Renaldi was satisfied, or left his kingdom, I was to continue with the matter in hand.

It is autumn now so I help Blanche in the garden, picking berries from the bushes, or helping her collect apples, peel them and prepare them for whatever concoction she wants to make. I love this season, brother, walking with her in the fields outside the city, watching the green leaves turn to gold, that last burst of light and life as summer dies. I don't know why. Perhaps it's Blanche's love of all that is natural, or maybe childhood memories, the woods and copses outside Newark, where father used to take us to play our battle games. He was always King Arthur, I Lancelot and, of course, as pious as ever, you had to be Sir Galahad. Memories, they always come back and roost in your soul. The older you become the more often it occurs. I always remember father's pendant, the gold locket hanging on a chain around his neck. How it would swing and glint in the sun as he bent down to listen to one of us. Take good care of it. Remember mother's wishes. Once you are gone, it is mine. I am not being avaricious, perhaps just maudlin, for with this task from the King, I find I drink more wine than perhaps is good for me. Anyway, I digress.

I used the time sheltering in my own house to list my doubts and thoughts about King Henry's death. First, I believe the King was murdered. But how? The abbot of Chertsey said blood was on the handle, not the blade of the dagger. And murder by whom? Surely Gloucester, and such an order could only have been given by King Edward himself? Secondly, why this hypocrisy? Oh, I understand the mischievous interference of Louis of France. But there must be something else? Thirdly, why was Ashby murdered? Why did he and Trollope visit the late King Henry? What passed between them? Fourthly, my mind keeps going back to it.

Why did King Henry, tainted with the possible bastardy of his own son, insinuate something scandalous about the House of York?

Of course, I reached no conclusion. Indeed, I began to wonder if I had been forgotten. I daydreamed about being left alone and that this task would disappear but my hopes were soon dashed. Early one Sunday morning Rokesley thundered on the door, shouting to be admitted. Blanche and I had just returned from church and we were planning a day of happy contentment but Rokesley ruined that.

'Clarence has been taken!' he shouted.

I ushered him to a stool in the buttery and sat down next to Blanche, holding her hand.

'What do you mean?' I whispered.

'Clarence has been arrested!' Rokesley repeated.

'On what charge?'

'High treason. Conspiracy, the use of the black arts, corresponding with the King's enemies beyond the seas.'

'But this is ridiculous,' I said. Yet I

remembered my visit to the Tower; the menacing atmosphere there and those long lines of dusty men-at-arms, trooping like shadows through the dust. Clarence had already been marked down for capture then. So what had happened? I studied Rokesley carefully. He was pale-faced, excited, but there was something in his eyes. Was it pleasure? Happiness at a prince's downfall from favour? I poured him a goblet of wine.

'Tell me,' I said, 'the full story.'

'It would appear,' Rokesley began, 'that our noble prince Clarence still entertained hopes of the crown. He had been in secret correspondence with Louis the Eleventh of France with a view to marrying Mary of Burgundy. He hoped that such an alliance would provide him with the men and resources to seize the English throne. Louis himself told our King this.'

'So,' I interrupted, 'Clarence may well have lent his weight to the French King's petition that Henry the Sixth be canonised?' Rokesley smiled and nodded.

'Correct. But he is guilty of more than

that. Ashby's death.'

'What do you mean?'

Rokesley looked up and took a deep breath.

'Clarence was confined to the Tower two days ago but, before that, King Edward ordered the arrest of certain of Clarence's household. They were taken to the Tower and put to the question.'

'You mean tortured?' I snapped.

'Well, yes, one of these, an Oxford clerk, John Stacey, was accused of sorcery. He broke down, confessed and named as an accomplice Thomas Burdett. Burdett was hanged the following day, he admitted to circulating evil writings and attempted to procure the King's death by necromancy. He also admitted to the murder of Ashby. His confession can be read in the court's roll.'

'Why did he kill Ashby?'

'Ashby was part of the conspiracy, he eventually threatened to go and confess all to the authorities.'

'I suppose Burdett also incriminated Clarence?'

'Yes,' Rokesley replied. 'Clarence was

not only negotiating with the French but spreading false rumours about his brother, the King.'

'What rumours?'

'Oh, how Edward had been born out of England. How he was not really the son of Richard of York but the bastard child of someone else. Clarence therefore argued that the King's children were illegitimate and could not succeed to the throne so, by right, the crown should go to him.'

I stared at Rokesley. What he told me in my own house that day made sense: Clarence had probably asked Louis to petition for the canonisation of Henry the Sixth in order to embarrass his own brother. He hated the Woodville woman, Edward's wife. Ashby, his priest, may have been part of the conspiracy and the rumours about Edward of York being of bastard issue may well have been what Henry the Sixth told Ashby in the Tower.

'So,' I asked, 'does our commission continue?'

'Of course. Renaldi insists on it.'

'Tell me, how did Clarence's treason come to light?'

'The Duke's conduct became more and more rash,' Rokesley replied.

I remembered Clarence bursting into my own house and nodded my head in agreement.

'Well,' Rokesley continued, 'Clarence gathered followers in his halls. He sent servants throughout the land to declare how the King dabbled in the black arts and poison. He said his brother the King meant to consume him as a candle consumes its own flame. He told his retainers to be ready in harness to levy outright war against the King. King Edward heard of all this, summoned Clarence to appear before him and, on the basis of confessions provided by the torturers as well as the information from royal spies, confined Clarence to the Tower.'

'Why do you tell us all this?' Blanche interrupted quietly. Rokesley grimaced.

'Well, for a number of reasons. First, we do know Clarence visited you in your own home, Master Physician. Secondly, you were seen talking to Trollope, the lawyer. Unfortunately he, too, was implicated in this conspiracy, being a former member of Clarence's household.'

Rokesley stopped and stared chillingly at me. I felt Blanche's hand clasp mine as a strange coldness clutched my body in its grip. Of all disease, treason is the most dangerous and deadly. You can be infected and not even know and be guilty by implication or association. I steadied my breathing and gazed back at Rokesley. Was he going to accuse me? Was I to be summoned? Is that why he had come? His sombre face suddenly broke into a grin. He leaned forward and patted me gently on the hand.

'Master Physician, I both tease and taunt you. Your name was raised by Richard of Gloucester but the Queen and I spoke for your lawyer. Nothing has been ascribed to you. I am right am I not?'

'Of course, you are!' I snapped back. 'Ask Trollope!' Rokesley grinned.

'We would like to. He was named by Burdett but, unfortunately, he has disappeared. There is a warrant out for his arrest.'

'Our commission gets smaller and smaller,' I quipped back. 'First Ashby, now Trollope. who will be next I wonder?' Rokesley stood up and dusted his gown.

'Nonsense, Luke, apply your logic. The King wanted this commission appointed. Clarence, for his own mischievous purposes, ensured two of his retainers were nominated. Now they are gone. We can reach our speedy conclusion that Henry the Sixth was a feckless man and an inept ruler, receive the grateful thanks of a generous King and go back, richly rewarded, to our own business.'

Rokesley smiled dazzlingly at Blanche as he tapped me on the shoulder.

'Your husband is well thought of, my Lady. Who knows how high he will climb. A knighthood? Lands? The trusted confidence of a King?'

Rokesley's flattery soothed away the anger in Blanche's eyes. Something stirred in me, a recklessness, a rebellion, a distaste for Rokesley's patronising ways. Who was he? I looked at him. Yes, who was he? Where did Rokesley come from? He smiled at me, I saw the concern in his eyes and felt guilty. The man had saved me, spoken highly of me and all I could do was be churlish in reply. I clasped him by the hand.

'Simon, you are right. But what shall we do now?'

'The commission sits again. Tonight,' he replied. I ignored Blanche's sigh of exasperation.

'You are to be there in the Star Chamber of Westminster Palace, about eight o'clock. The King will expect you.' He bowed, took his leave and left more quietly than he had arrived.

Blanche and I spent the rest of the day discussing the news which was now common report in the streets of the city. Clarence was arrested. Clarence was in the Tower. Clarence had fallen, like Lucifer, never to rise again. Blanche could not stop talking, excited by the sudden news and the contrasts of Rokesley's words from hinting that I might be a traitor to promises of rapid advancement.

By evening, I was relieved to be out of the house, glad to be alone in the cool night air. This time I went armed with sword, dagger and club and roused one of my apprentices, the eldest and boldest, to carry a lantern horn before me. Blanche became anxious but I explained how Clarence's arrest may cause tumults in the streets and surely the life of her husband was precious?

As soon as I was within the palace, leaving my apprentice outside to chat and talk with other retainers, I could feel the strain caused by Clarence's fall. The corridors and passageways were ghostly, empty, the few people I met frightened and subdued. At every turn and corner, Edward had placed professional soldiers or knights from his own household in full harness and armour. They stood beneath the flickering cresset torches, stirring now and again, menacing threat in every mailed movement. A court usher stopped and asked me my business. I told him and, in hushed tones he ordered me to follow him, up a staircase to a heavily guarded, iron-studded door. Again more questions. A knight banneret, a young man, made all the more threatening by the chain mail coif round his head and the naked sword in his hand, reluctantly allowed me through. Inside, the Star Chamber room was a feast of light and warmth. The gold stars on the blue painted wall reflected the light of a hundred pure wax candles fixed in their holders. The group on the dais around the huge oak table stopped speaking as I entered. I recognised the King and immediately genuflected, head bowed.

'Oh, come on, Master Luke!' he called out. 'Do not let us stand on idle ceremony. Now you are here, we can proceed apace.' I acknowledged the soft rebuke for being late but I made no apology. My rebelliousness had returned. I resented the cowed feeling about the palace and why I, an innocent person, should be frightened of anything. I took my seat and gazed around. Elizabeth the Queen was there next to her husband, her face as beautiful as ever though her large eyes looked troubled and anxious.

On the other side of Edward sat Renaldi, studying the rings on his fingers, quiet, impassive, as if trying to distance himself from the scandal which had surfaced at the English court.

Further down the table Gloucester, his thin white face hard and bleak, the eyes more hooded than ever. The only time I saw him move was to look down the table at the Queen. I flinched at the pure hatred I saw in his eyes. Across from me Rokesley, nodding and smiling and half-rising when I took my seat beside Gough, who did not even bother to acknowledge my presence. He slouched, constantly watching his master Gloucester.

Of all those present, Edward seemed the least perturbed, making no reference to Clarence but insisting that each of us report on what progress we had made. Trollope was never referred to. I shivered, it was as if the lawyer had never existed.

Rokesley spoke enthusiastically, nothing really new had been found. Gough repeated his story in a monotone, showing his distaste for the task. I told what I could, being evasive about those matters I thought did not concern them. Edward smilingly heard us all out. I do

136

think he would have brought the matter to an end there and then but, Renaldi, a look of mischief in his eyes, suddenly stirred.

'Your Grace,' he said softly. 'I have to answer to my masters. What you are saying is that there are no grounds for the canonisation of the late King Henry. But,' he coughed, 'and I mean no offence, I am talking to people who had every reason to oppose King Henry. In other words, my sources are biased. His Holiness did not spend good silver and gold sending me here simply to report back what you want me to tell him.'

'What more do you want?' Gloucester interrupted. 'What can we do?'

'We can listen to His Eminence,' the Queen answered tartly, disdaining to even look at her brother-in-law.

'His Holiness,' Gloucester answered, 'can ask for what he wants. But in this kingdom his authority is limited to matters ecclesiastical and spiritual. He has no authority to send subjects of the King hither and thither, asking questions about a man who should never have been allowed to rule in the first place.'

Renaldi smiled.

'I shall inform His Holiness of His Grace, the Duke's observation. But, as I said, I make no criticism. I simply ask for your help in carrying out a task assigned to me.'

Perhaps I was tired of the banter and so spoke up before anyone could stop me.

'Your Grace,' I said to the King. 'There is one thing we can do.'

Edward raised his eyebrows.

'Perhaps we can help the papal legate. The corpse of the late King Henry lies at Chertsey Abbey. It should be,' I continued in a rush, watching Gloucester react angrily, 'be exhumed and examined. I believe that is the offical procedure in the Roman Church's process of canonisation.'

Renaldi beamed at me as if I was a long lost friend but I glimpsed the good humour fade from the King's eyes.

'Is that so, Your Eminence?' he asked. Renaldi nodded.

'It is. A procedure laid down by Canon Law. Let me give you an example.

Recently the Church investigated the life of a saintly monk, his body was exhumed. When the lid of the coffin was taken off, the deep score marks of his nails were found on the lid.' Renaldi did not stop speaking, even at the Queen's gasp of horror. 'It was obvious,' he continued, 'the poor man had been buried alive. He had later regained consciousness and attempted to free himself from his tomb. The process of canonisation stopped because the presiding official declared the poor man may have despaired and so lost the chance of sanctity.' On any other occasion I would have condemned such stupid harshness out of hand but I nodded as Renaldi spoke. The King rubbed his mouth on the back of his hand before flicking his fingers as a sign for his wine cup to be filled. The Queen herself served him, leaning over the table in a gust of costly perfume and the rustle of expensive silks. Edward drank greedily, his eyes hard, his mind searching for an answer. He slammed the cup down on the table and smiled.

'I agree,' he said. He looked at his

brother. 'Gloucester, you supervise this.' He clapped Renaldi hard on the shoulder. 'Of course, our friend, His Eminence, will be present, as will be our physician, Luke. Doctors very rarely help the living, perhaps he can do something for a dead man!' He grinned at me to show he meant no malice and, bellowing with laughter, swept out of the room.

We all began to leave: Gloucester and Gough going to stand in a corner by the door, talking in hushed tones. Rokesley patted me gently on the arm, as if approving of what I had said. The Queen came up and took me by the hand. I felt her skin warm as velvet, soft as shot silk and I wondered again about the rumours. Elizabeth had been married before, a widow when King Edward met her. They say she trapped him by witchcraft and I half believed them as I gazed into her large, dark eyes. Their colour seemed to change according to her mood; on that sombre night, they were large dark pools, full of intense passion.

'Luke,' she said. 'I welcome your advice. Let this matter be finished so you can rejoin my household. We miss you.' She turned, went back to the table and picked up her own goblet, pure silver, the stem crusted with rubies and other precious stones. Elizabeth pressed the cup into my hand.

'Here, Luke,' she said. 'Take this. A gift for you. A token of our appreciation.'

She drew from her belt a small purse which she emptied into the cup so the pile of silver coins winked and glittered like some rare, exotic drink.

'A present for your wife,' she whispered. She clutched my wrist; 'Sad times, Luke, perilous, dangerous ones. I still fear Clarence's vicious tongue. If you hear such rumours, inform me, tell Rokesley.'

I glimpsed the panic in her eyes and wondered what she meant. I remembered stories, scurrilous gossip, of how the King's attentions were beginning to wander. I idly wondered if Clarence's real treason was to drive a wedge between Edward and his wife, a woman Clarence had always hated. The Queen touched me gently on the cheek and followed her husband out of the room, Rokesley in close attendance.

I picked up my own cloak and made to leave, so lost in my own thoughts I was startled to find the door barred by Gloucester. The Duke stood, legs apart, one shoulder raised higher than the other as he brushed his ear against the thick, black velvet of his jerkin. His thin lips bared into a smile which never reached his eyes. On his left, deeper in the shadows, stood Gough watching silently, the ever faithful mastiff.

'Your Grace,' I asked, 'you have business with me?' Gloucester straightened and came closer, the red flush of anger high in his cheeks. He clutched the hilt of his dagger strapped to his belt, pulling it in and out restlessly as if wanting to draw it and release the anger pent up within him.

'Yes,' he mimicked in reply. 'His Grace has business with you!'

'Then I am your servant,' I replied coolly.

Gloucester laid one hand on my shoulder.

'Oh no, not me,' he answered in mock

surprise. 'His Grace, the Duke of Clarence.'

'Clarence is in the Tower,' I retorted. 'He is the King's prisoner. I have no business with him.' Fear churned my belly. 'Your Grace,' I said hurriedly, 'I do not wish to be seen with Clarence and have some accusation levelled against me of complicity or collusion in his treasons.'

'Tush, man,' Gloucester patted me on the shoulder. 'You have my protection. Clarence fears the Queen may poison him. He wishes you to advise him and ensure the pains in his belly are due to poor victuals, rather than some venomous potion. Indeed, you have no choice in the matter. You are under my protection and at my command.' He turned and stared out of the mullion-glassed window. 'It is dark,' he continued in a whisper. 'Perhaps it would be best now.' He turned back. 'You will come?' I spread my hands.

'Your Grace, as I said, I am your servant.'

We left the chamber, Gough scurrying ahead of Richard, who was joined by other valets and squires from his household. We made our way out of the palace, down to the King's Steps, where a huge eight-oared barge lay waiting. A cold wind ruffled the dark choppy water of the Thames. My unease and panic grew as mailed men clambered in the barge with us. As it pulled away from the bank, another barge, also full of armed men wearing Gloucester's livery, stood awaiting amid-stream to accompany us down to the Tower. The journey was made in total silence, Gloucester and Gough lounging in their seats, the men-at-arms around us impassive and cold. No sound except the slop of the water, the clink of armour and the distant, heart-wrenching noises of the night creatures on the far river bank. Above us, a hunter's moon slid in and out of the clouds, its pale light reflected in the waters. The oarsmen of both barges pulled lustfully. We seemed to skim across the surface of the river like some eerie bird of the night hunting its prey.

At the Tower, both the quayside and the fortress were heavily guarded but

Gloucester swept through, the sight of his face and the presence of his armed retainers sufficient authority. Inside the gateway, every passageway and tunnel was lit by flickering pitch torches placed high in the wall. On the battlements, archers walking to and fro, cross-bows loaded. I trembled for Clarence. If the Duke thought his brother would relent he was mistaken. Clarence was confined for what remained of his life. The King was determined to block any attempts to rescue his faithless brother. I smiled dourly as we were taken up to Clarence's prison chamber, the same room as the late King Henry had used. Now the staircase was heavily guarded; three men-at-arms, their swords drawn, stood at the top, the door to the chamber padlocked at least three times. Again Gloucester rapped out his orders. There was a rustle of keys, the sound of locks being pulled back and Gloucester, taking me by the arm, ushered me into the room.

Last time the room had been stark and empty but now attempts had been made to recognise the status of the prisoner; clean rushes on the floor, drapes covered the walls and charcoal braziers, piled high with gleaming perfumed coals, stood around the room. Clarence was waiting for us, sitting nonchalantly on the corner of the table. He rose as we entered. He smiled mischievously at his brother and waved me to the chamber's one and only chair. He filled two flagons of wine, gave one to me whilst he sat on the bed opposite. Gloucester he now ignored. Clarence toasted both of us and sipped appreciatively from the cup.

'The best Malmesey,' he said. 'My favourite.' He turned. 'Richard, I beg you, please leave us alone. I wish to talk with my visitor.'

At first I thought Gloucester was going to refuse but then, he grimaced, gave a silent shrug, and left the chamber.

'My Lord,' I said hastily, for Clarence bowed his head, his air of bravado quite gone. 'You wished to speak to me? You are frightened of poison?'

Clarence shook his head and looked up, the tears brimming in his eyes and a pained look which removed all the arrogance from his face.

'I am not afraid of dying,' he whispered, 'One way is as good as another. I am to die am I not?'

'I cannot say, my Lord. I do not have the ear of the King. Ask your brother!'

'No one will tell me anything,' Clarence replied.

'They accuse you of treason, my Lord.'

'You mean the Queen and her brood of Woodvilles!' Clarence angrily retorted. 'Oh, yes, they mean to see me dead. Because of what I know.'

'And what is that?' I asked.

Clarence crossed his arms as if he was hugging some secret to himself.

'My Lord, what do you know? Is it that you want to tell me?'

Clarence looked up slyly beneath his eyebrows.

'There's something wrong,' he whispered. 'Did Ashby ever talk to you?'

'No, my Lord.'

Clarence looked towards the door.

'Well, the late King Henry spoke to him,' he whispered. 'Something dreadful, so Ashby told me but you know the priests. They talk about the seal of confession. I asked if he had said anything to anyone else. Ashby replied, 'Bishop Stillington of Bath and Wells had the half of it.' You know Stillington?'

Of course I did. The Bishop, a trained lawyer, was Chancellor of the realm until King Edward dismissed him.

'Why should he tell Stillington anything?' I asked.

'Two reasons. First, Stillington was a lawyer. Secondly, according to Canon Law, Ashby came from the west country. He was a native of Stillington's diocese and so under his jurisdiction.'

'What did he mean by Stillington knowing the half of it?'

'I don't know,' Clarence replied. 'But when I pressed him further, and he was a man who loved to play with words, Ashby simply quoted the Latin tag — 'Carpe Diem', Seize the Day.' I stirred in my seat.

'But surely what Ashby said did not bring you here, my Lord? On a charge of treason?'

Clarence shrugged, brushing the dust from his dark woollen hose.

'Oh, there's really nothing else,' he replied sourly. 'I did some stupid things. Spoke my mind, plotted and conspired. I armed my retainers for I was frightened of the Woodvilles. I believe the Queen wants me dead.'

I thought of the Queen's heart-shaped face and beautiful eyes.

'But, my Lord, that's untrue. Why should the Queen want that?'

'Ah!' Clarence let out a deep sigh and leaned back. 'Not because of what I have done, not because of what I have said but, perhaps, because what she suspects I know.'

'And what is that, my Lord?'

'Ah, there's the riddle. I don't know it though I have been trying to find out.'

I looked at Clarence's flushed face and gleaming eyes. My skill is with the body, very rarely do I touch the mind, but I thought him mad and remembered rumours I had heard about the court.

Wasn't Clarence's own son a simpleton? Had the boy inherited his father's madness? I rose.

'My Lord, is that why you asked to see me? I mean, if Ashby had told me anything?'

Clarence nodded and I saw the deep disappointment in his eyes.

'My Lord,' I said slowly. 'They say you killed Ashby because he wanted to reveal your so-called treason.' Clarence laughed sourly.

'Nonsense! I suppose Trollope, too, has been implicated?'

'Yes, my Lord.'

'Nonsense!' he whispered. 'True, they were my retainers. I ensured they were members of Renaldi's blessed commission. Their only crime was to act as my mediators with Henry the Sixth, though Trollope admitted that came to nothing. Henry refused to talk to him though I believe he made a confession to Ashby the priest.' Clarence looked at me.

'My Lord,' I repeated. 'He told me nothing.'

'A pity,' Clarence murmured. 'For the

150

King says if I made a full confession, he would grant me a pardon.'

'I have one question, my Lord,' I said, 'before I go. This is the very cell where King Henry the Sixth died.'

Clarence looked up slyly.

'My Lord, do you know anything about his death?'

Clarence threw himself back, laughing dementedly.

'No, I do not!' he shouted. 'For that night I was drunk on malmesey. Ask my brother Gloucester! Capable, efficient Gloucester! I think he should tell you everything. Now go!'

I turned and hammered on the door. Gloucester swung it open and I was grateful to be out, leaving Clarence giggling like a maniac. Gloucester went before me downstairs; outside, the donjon was now ringed by armed men, made all the more awesome by the flickering torches they carried. Gloucester took me by the elbow through their ranks into the shadow of some trees.

'My brother is well?' he asked.

'Your brother is frightened.'

'What did he ask you?'

'If Ashby had spoken to me,' I replied.

'Did he?'

'No, Your Grace.'

Gloucester rubbed his mouth with his hand and looked back towards the Tower.

'What is it?' he murmured, as if to himself. 'What is it Clarence wants to know?'

He looked sharply back at me.

'You are telling the truth?'

'I am, Your Grace. But I have one question for you. I came here to the Tower on your orders. I have done what you asked. But now I ask you, as a King's Commissioner, what do you know of the death of Henry the Sixth? You were in his chamber when the guards came to collect his body.'

Gloucester smiled, this time genuinely, no artifice. Perhaps he admired my courage, I don't know.

'I tell you this,' he replied. He half raised his hand as if swearing an oath. 'I swear on the sacrament, I was not involved in his death. On the evening he died, my brothers and I were here, in the royal apartments. Clarence was drunk, perhaps that was why the King sent for me. He took me aside and told me something was wrong. I was to go to the Wakefield Tower. I was not to ask any questions but to act on what I saw and never mention it again.' He paused and coughed. 'I came across, there were no guards and the door to Henry's chamber was unlocked. Inside, the late King sat slumped against the wall, head forward, eyes closed. I examined the body. The skull at the back of the head was smashed, there was blood on the chamber wall. I reached the conclusion that Henry of Lancaster, having heard about the defeat of his wife and the death of his son, had taken his own life by dashing his head against the wall.'

'Is that possible?' I asked. 'Really, Your Grace?' Gloucester shrugged.

'I have asked physicians. They say it is more than possible and, if Henry had a thin skull, only one blow need suffice. You are a physician, Master Luke, judge for yourself.'

At the time I agreed. Some men have

fragile bones. One man can take a knock on the head and walk away unscathed, yet another will drop dead if hit by a ball of mud.

Gloucester now seemed impatient to go. Unwilling to continue the conversation, he would have dismissed me and let me make my own way back but then he called after me.

'Master Luke, I brought you here. The least I can do is ensure your safe return.'

Three soldiers were ordered to accompany me and we entered the main gate just past the portcullis when a shadow loomed up and lunged at me. My escort grabbed him, hustling him out into the light.

'Do you recognise him?' one of them asked gruffly.

'No,' I replied. I looked closer, the fellow was drunk. He wore the livery of a Tower guard, although this was stained with cheap wine and beer so he stank like an alehouse. I went up and grasped the man's face between my hands.

'Why did you attack me?' I asked.

The man looked blearily back.

'Cantrone!' he muttered, mouthing curses. 'Cantrone was safe until you talked to him. Now he is dead. His throat was cut and tossed into the river as if he was rubbish!'

I thought of the young soldier and groaned to myself. The drunk was right, it was no coincidence that Cantrone died after I had spoken to him.

'Listen, man,' I said hoarsely. 'I swear on the sacrament that Cantrone's death cannot be laid at my door.' I looked at the escort. 'Let him go!' I ordered. They shrugged and threw him to one side where he collapsed like a bundle of rags and we continued our journey.

I was relieved to be home for Cantrone's death bothered me. Was I the real cause for his murder? But who had seen me speak to him? Cantrone must have gossiped with other members of the garrison and there would be spies. Yet, the day I had seen Cantrone, Gloucester had been in the Tower. Was the silent, devious Duke responsible for this?

My troubles only increased when I opened the door and Blanche came down. I never have seen her in such a rage.

'You slink about,' she shouted, 'like some alley cur and do not tell me where you go or what you do! I am not a child. I know this business troubles you.'

I showed her the Queen's gift but she threw it aside angrily.

'Try not to buy me with sweetmeats!' she said. 'But tell me, as your wife, what is happening. I am not some princess from one of Chaucer's tales.'

'More like the wife of Bath!' I retorted, and ducked as Blanche picked up the cup the Queen had given and sent it flying at my head. At last she calmed and sat down angrily on a chair, kicking at the rushes with one sandalled foot as if they, not me, were responsible for her present unhappiness. I knew she was right. I crouched beside her and told her, faltering at first, exactly what was happening, becoming secretly alarmed as I saw fear replace anger in her face. When I had finished talking I just sat there, Blanche staring down at the floor.

'This is dangerous, Luke,' she murmured. 'So dangerous for both of us. You are told to seek out one thing yet we know it is only the cover for greater mysteries.' She grabbed me by the hand. 'Forget your degrees and training, your knowledge and the respect people have for you. We are small people, the little ones of the land. Let Clarence die. Let Gloucester move in the shadows. You only live, Luke, because they want you to. You are playing a game blind-folded, staggering about in the dark. God knows what traps you could fall into.'

I stopped her protests with a kiss and led her upstairs to our own chamber. I know she is right. But what can I do? I wish you would write, Stephen, and advise me. I tell you, as I told Blanche, every word, every nuance, each look and gesture. Perhaps that is my mistake. I should examine more carefully what is happening. I wish I could write to you as I used to do before about Blanche, my work, my friends, my hopes and dreams. Pray for me. God keep you. Luke.

Written 20th October 1477.

Letter 5

Luke, Physician, to Brother Stephen, monk at Aylesford Priory in Kent. Health and greetings.

Sweet Christ, and I mean no blasphemy, but let me get rid of all the courtesies and courtly conventions. We are brothers. Indeed, you are my confessor. I can tell you what happens for, despite Blanche's determined appeal to tell her the truth, how can I? This matter is now muddy and murky like some stagnant pool, calm and still on the surface but, once stirred, all the evil vapours and dirt rise to the top. Or, like some city whore, clothed in her paint and gilted garb but the white paint disguises sores, and the carmine lips hide rows of blackened teeth. So, too, with this business. Perhaps it was Clarence's words or maybe my argument with Blanche or the death of Cantrone but a week after I wrote my last letter to you, Stephen, I spent days listing what I knew.

The danger had begun with Ashby's sudden death. Strange, one night I dreamt of him. A nightmare. An evil phantasm brought by some succubus or other demon from hell. I was on a wild, desolate plain, the ground a fine white sand, the sky purple-red. In the middle of this plain was a huge castle built of iron, its windows empty and across a draw-bridge a massive door which kept swinging open and shut. I went in and along a darkened passageway and found myself in a chamber. I thought the walls were covered in velvet but found, on closer inspection, that they were the living bodies of rats massed together. In my dream I sat down at a table, long and dark, either end stretching into infinity. In the middle of this table stood a huge jar of pure glass filled with water, the kind used to put some morsel or organ cut from a body but in my nightmare, the glass was large enough to take a man's corpse. I saw Ashby floating there, his face pressed against the glass, eyes staring and wisps of hair streaming round him like some shabby halo: fat lips opening and shutting like the fish in the pond he was drowned in. He was shouting at me but I could not hear. I wanted to free him but I could not move. His hands beat against the glass as his face took on a mottled hue. I felt every gasp he took as if my own breath was being cut away.

I woke sweating and screaming. Blanche could not comfort me, so I rose and went downstairs to my own chamber. I poured a goblet of wine and sat in the darkness. I remembered Santander, a Morisco physician from Cordobo who had laughingly dismissed dreams as signs or warnings, stroking his goatee beard, he smilingly protested how most dreams are caused by humours which rise from what we eat or, in the case of those who see visions, what we do not eat. However, he added, dreams are often our cares or anxieties which come back to haunt us. Sitting in my chamber I believed he was right for something about Ashby's death had always troubled me. Clarence did not murder him yet his death was no accident, then the solution came to me.

Ashby's body had been in the water, face down, cold, but the cup of mulled wine beside him was warm to the touch.

I jumped up and went back to the buttery, telling one of the maids who slept under a small trestle bed in the corner, not to worry but go back to sleep whilst I re-kindled the fire. Soon the flames flared into life. I poured some wine into a pewter goblet and brought it near the fire, placing two small pokers into the flames. I left them there until they glowed red hot and plunged them immediately into the pewter cup. Once again I did it until the wine became boiling hot to the touch. I took a rag, wrapped it round the goblet and took it back to my chamber, asking the maid to excuse the madness of her master and take a pot of water to extinguish the fire.

In my chamber I placed the mulled wine on a table and, taking an hour glass, turned it over, watching the sand trickle through. I took into consideration how Ashby's cup had been out in the open near cold water and I surmised that my cup became as warm to the touch as

Ashby's in a very short while, perhaps five or seven minutes after the hour glass had first been turned. My conclusions were as simple and as clear as any of Euclid's theories. First, Ashby had taken that wine cup out. He must have therefore not expected danger from someone whom he trusted and wanted to talk to in the garden. Secondly, Ashby had put the wine cup down on the low bench near his carp pond; his visitor, however, had wasted no time. He wrapped the noose round the priest's neck, extinguishing Ashby's life like the flame of a guttering candle and had cleverly thrown the corpse into the pond. A subtle stratagem. Any physician or coroner, even the stupidest, (and I say this as no apology for my own foolishness) can tell how long a man has been dead from the warm texture of his skin but with Ashby this was not possible. The pond water had been icy cold and any body warmth soon gone. Finally, the murderer must have known (and again I do not mean to boast) that a physician of my learning and skill would soon be there. Hence the immersion of Ashby's corpse in the water.

I smiled ruefully. All this proved was that Ashby had been murdered and, secondly, that the murder had something to do with Ashby's work but just what? I thought of Ashby's teasing words to Clarence. What had he said? 'Bishop Stillington knew the half of it.' I could make nothing of that. But what else? The Latin tag. 'Carpe Diem?' Suddenly I knew what Ashby had meant. So clear, so perfectly understandable that I guffawed with laughter so loud as to arouse one of my apprentices in the adjoining room.

I was so excited I couldn't sleep and, as soon as it was dawn, the city bells clanging for Mass, I dressed hurriedly. I gulped down some watered ale between mouthfuls of rye bread and hurried out into Cheapside, I pushed aside anyone who impeded my progress; beggars, apprentice boys, roisterers, still half drunk, even members of the city watch. I reached the Guildhall but its doors were still locked and sealed so I had to kick my heels in a nearby church, watching some priest drone the last words of the dawn

Mass. Eventually the Hall was opened and, using my royal warrants, I demanded in a loud voice the whereabouts of the coroner. I scurried along passageways, upstairs, stopping half-awakened servants, shouting my questions at them. The commotion I caused attracted two tipstaffs. They hurried up to me, dressed in the city livery, their white batons of office clenched in their hands as if they were wands which could make me disappear.

'You, sir,' one of them barked. 'The tumult you cause.'

'And you, sir!' I said, stepping closer, pulling out one of the royal warrants, 'are impeding a messenger from the King.' The man's face went as white as his wand of office. He glimpsed the ornate seal and stepped back.

'My apologies,' he stuttered, 'but how can I, we help?' I smiled and told him and, within minutes, I was ushered into Master Coroner's office as if I was the Chancellor himself. The coroner looked up angrily from behind a heap of documents.

'Master Coroner,' I began. 'You do remember me?' The coroner gazed blankly back. 'The priest, John Ashby,' I said. 'The one found drowned in his carp pond some weeks ago.' A look of recognition dawned in the fellow's eyes. He pursed his lips and drew himself up.

'Ah, yes,' he replied. 'The house is still sealed,' he declared. 'The priest died intestate. There is some question of who inherits the property, the relatives, the church?' He smiled thinly. 'Or should the King seize all his chattels?'

'I am not interested in that,' I snapped back, regretting my anger as the man narrowed his eyes. A hard man. Why does power affect such people? I hid my own impatience. 'Look,' I said, 'I sympathise with you, sir, but you have unearthed no evidence about the priest's murder?'

The coroner shook his head.

'No,' he answered. 'In fact, I was going to question you and the others who were there at the house. I don't really care if you are the King's commissioners. This is London, sir, and any crime committed within its walls must be investigated by

the sheriffs and properly-appointed coro-
ners of the city.' He sat back, sticking out
his chest as if I should be humbled by
such a pompous proclamation. I nodded
ingratiatingly. The fellow was now in full
flow, borne along by his own self
importance.

'Yes, sir,' he said. 'I wanted to question
you and the others. Not only about that
crime but about the other one.'

'Which?' I asked, though I suspected
the answer.

'The house was ransacked!' he
snapped. 'Room by room. The seals of the
city broken.' He quivered in anger.

'A terrible crime,' I cried in mock
alarm. 'But who could have done this?'

'No ordinary burglar or housebreaker.
Valuables were left. Whoever the felons
may be, they were looking for something.
Only God knows if they found it!'

'Master Coroner,' I replied, drawing
closer. 'I believe I may have evidence
which will help you not only seize the
murderer of John Ashby but also the
scoundrel who scorned your seals with
such impunity. I can give you information

which will bring you to the notice, not only of the city fathers but even of the King himself.'

Oh, Stephen, the greed of men! Their love of power and the sweet poison of flattery. The fellow positively beamed at me.

'I ask for your help,' I whispered. 'I need to go to Ashby's house alone.' The fellow was about to draw back. 'No, not in the building,' I said, 'but the garden. I cannot tell you why but, soon, I promise you.'

The man's eyes searched mine. He bit his lip as if he was about to refuse but changed his humour and walked back into his small chamber. A short while later he returned with a slip of parchment bearing the Coroner's seal.

'This,' he announced grandly, 'will give you access into the garden. Show it to the city watch on guard there. They will allow you in. But, sir, remember, I look forward to your report.'

I thanked him profusely, heaping one assurance upon another. I quietly vowed to myself that I would be crowned Sultan of the Turks before I did this pompous fool's bidding.

'Oh, one other matter,' I said as the man turned away. 'This may interest you. The lawyer, Trollope, he is missing. He may well be the murderer. He is also accused of treason. Sir, I beg you to look through the city death lists and see if any corpse has been found which fits his description.'

I gave the Coroner details of Trollope's appearance which he memorised, eyes closed, lips pursed.

'What makes you think he is dead?' he asked.

I shrugged.

'He may have taken his own life,' I answered, 'or his accomplices, believing he knew too much, may have done away with him.'

After that I left the Guildhall. God knows why I had asked about Trollope. I did not even know if I told the truth. Trollope may have been the murderer but I had this strange feeling he was dead. I walked back to Candlewick Street. A fine day, though I kept my hood up over my head for I did not wish to be recognised and I had (and still have) a deep unease about being followed. At Ashby's house, the usual city bully boys were on guard, officious and half-drunk even though it was early in the morning. After some coarse jests, they let me through the side entrance into Ashby's garden, now overgrown, though even I could see it had been pillaged: the apple and pear trees completely stripped of their fruit, the vegetable and herb gardens uprooted. Of course, the carp pond was now empty of water. The fish probably stolen for sale in the market or to provide some city guard with a splendid supper. All that was left was a huge bowl of rotting mud and the sluice gate at the bottom hacked from its hinges, the water long drained into some underground river or sewer.

I stepped gingerly down, my boots slipping on the mud-encrusted rocks. The pond, when full, would have been well over a man's height and I had to take care as I walked around, studying the grey stone sides of the fishery. I began to despair. The bricks were all in place, the cement and mortar between them undisturbed. I spent well over an hour before my search was rewarded. A small loose stone, a hand's breadth across. I seized it and gently pulled it out. I put my hand in the hole, cold and dank, but I found it. A small leather pouch which I eagerly grasped and immediately hid beneath my robes. I replaced the stone and managed to heave myself out of the mud.

I left the garden looking disgruntled, giving the guards the impression that my search had been futile. Once back home, however, I ignored even Blanche and hurried to my own chamber. The leather pouch had been securely sealed at the neck and I had to use a knife to cut the red twine. The parchment inside had been kept dry by its oil-soaked leather covering. About a foot long, six inches wide, sharply cut down one edge like some indenture or agreement. Whatever Ashby had written he had cut in half, retaining one portion and sending the other to his own bishop, Stillington of Bath and Wells. Clarence had unwittingly led me to this. By the pun 'Carpe Diem',

Ashby was referring to his own carp pond and his other phrase, 'Bishop Stillington has the half of it', neatly explained the whereabouts of the other part of this important document which had cost Ashby his life. I shivered for it may cost me the same. Perhaps it was the reason why Henry the Sixth had died and could well prove to be Clarence's death warrant.

I lit a candle and studied this death-bearing document and gasped with astonishment. The mauve handwriting was clear but it meant nothing. Strange signs and hieroglyphics. Words from the Greek alphabet but they made no sense to me. Ashby had written them out for the letters were well formed, beautifully set out in a clerk's hand. But what did they mean? I spent hours, days trying to understand Ashby's memorandum. But nothing, nothing at all so I explained to Blanche that I had to leave. She was to tell no one where I had gone. I bought a horse from the market at Smithfield, hired a sumpter pony and, early one morning, left the city by Aldgate and took the road west to Bath.

My journey was uneventful. I travelled by day, ensuring I always had companions: a party of merchants, some Welsh scholars returning home from Oxford; a travelling troupe of actors, their creaking carts full of strange costumes and devices which they would set up in some town or village to entertain the people. I made sure I was never alone. Yet the feeling of being pursued still dogged me as if some dark presence brooded over my journey. After three days on the road, I was grateful to enter the city of Bath. I confess, at first, I wandered amongst the markets there, looking at the geegaws and trinkets on sale. Bath was an old Roman colony and, God bless me, my aspirations were satisfied. Some old blackened coins were on sale. Strange, the gold of a mighty Roman emperor sold for a few pennies by some ragged tinker from his battered tray. Of course, I remembered the reason for my journey, brought home by a feeling of coldness down my back, a pricking between my shoulder blades, my hair curling on the nape of my neck. I felt like some guard dog who knew danger threatened but could not discover its source.

I went up to the Bishop's palace within the precincts of the cathedral. I gave some officious deacon my name and rank and showed him the royal warrants. After waiting for an hour or two I was ushered into the presence of the Bishop. Stillington's reputation as a lawyer only equalled that of a time-server who had once been trusted by King Edward until a sudden fall from power sent him scuttling back to tend his flock. Not the sort of shepherd I would trust, more interested in the fleece and the price it would fetch than the sheep.

I expected a wily politician and was not disappointed. Stillington may have fallen from power but he still kept its trappings. He sat enthroned, waiting for me behind a broad, oaken table. Oh, you priests! The Bishop, so his official told me, had just celebrated the mid-day Mass and now seemed intent on relaxing after his onerous priestly duties. His chamber was sweet-smelling like that of some rich old lady; rushes and crushed herbs on the floor, thick blue-gold tapestries covered the walls and shimmered in the light of scores of beeswax candles. The bishop's wealth was apparent in the cups, chalices, plates and dishes and other costly items scattered haphazardly round the spacious chamber. Stillington himself was intent on finishing a plate of pastries and guzzling greedily from a jewel-encrusted goblet. His voice was harsh and impatient as he ordered me forward to sit on a small stool beside his desk. I felt like some minor cleric about to be reproved for some moral misdemeanour. 'Deo gratias' I was not, I would not like Stillington to be my master. His great corpulent body, a mass of flesh beneath silk and sable robes. His face round, the jowls hanging down, glistening like those of a mastiff, the lips thin and bloodless, prim and bitter as any old maid's. On either side of his red, squat, spotty nose the eyes were small and dead, flat and lifeless like two raisins in a bowl of heavy dough. He studied me for a while, balancing the goblet in one hand.

'You are a physician? You're from the court?'

'Yes, my Lord,' I replied.

'You are here on the King's business?'

'You are correct, my Lord.'

Stillington smirked.

'The King, he sends messages?'

'No, my Lord. I am here on business connected with the King, though it may concern you, as it did one of your priests, John Ashby.'

Oh, Stephen, I was pleased at that. Stillington's jaw sagged, his mouth opening and shutting like one of poor Ashby's carps.

'My Lord,' I continued smoothly, 'let us be honest and not waste each other's time.' I was tired of the stupid little stool, so I stood up. 'Ashby knew some great secret did he not?'

Stillington, his face wary, nodded. 'He sent you a document, my Lord?'

Stillington just stared back. I drew the parchment from my own wallet.

'I believe, my Lord, you have the other half of this?'

Stillington, despite his size, moved

quickly, his hand snaking out. He would have snatched it from my grip but I hastily stepped back.

'No, my Lord. I want the other half.'

Stillington sat back in his chair.

'Why should I give it to you?' he said.

'Oh, for two reasons, my Lord. First, we can see what he wrote. Secondly, if you do not, I shall tell all I know to the King and, believe me, within days others much rougher will come to demand it of you.'

Stillington looked down at his jewel-encrusted fingers, splaying them out like the talons of some bird.

'I have the document,' he murmured, 'but it makes no sense to me.' He looked up. 'Of course, it is divided and I suppose yours is the other half?'

I nodded.

'So, how do we proceed?' he asked.

I sat back on the stool.

'My Lord, whatever that document contains killed Ashby. It will undoubtedly send Clarence to the scaffold. It may have been the decisive factor in the execution of the late King Henry the Sixth.' I saw the startled look of surprise on Stillington's face. 'Oh, yes, my Lord,' I continued, 'King Henry was murdered. A true martyr, a holy man, a saint, just as great, perhaps greater than Thomas a Beckett. Give me the other half of the document,' I said. 'Lock me in some chamber. I shall make a fair copy which I will leave with you. The original I will take. Whoever,' I lied, 'manages to extricate the secret of the document will communicate it to the other. We are agreed on that?'

The bishop nodded, rose and moved his great bulk across the room. He rummaged beneath his robes for a huge set of keys. He stopped, breathing noisily as he examined these, singled out three and unlocked the enormous chest in the far corner of the room. Each key had to be used before he could lift the lid. He took out a small wooden casket bound with iron hoops. Two more keys were selected, the lid prised open and Stillington showed me a leather pouch similar to the one I had found in Ashby's carp pond. This was bound and sealed at the neck with the Bishop's own signet ring. Stillington broke this, plucked out the manuscript and nonchalantly handed it over before wordlessly taking me into an adjoining chamber. The Bishop waved me to a small table and stool and brought me a writing tray, a cup of wine and a plate of thin sugared wafers. He looked at me, shrugged and left the chamber. I heard him turn the lock, sealing me in.

The bishop knew I could not escape, the room was airless, a small arrow slit window high in the wall and the heavy door was bolted. Of course, I did not drink the wine or touch the wafers. Only a fool or a drunkard would have run the risk of being quietly drugged, the manuscript stolen whilst I could be murdered and dumped in some city ditch. I spent the rest of the day transcribing the manuscript, each side carefully copied. The letters were Greek. Ashby must have been a classical scholar with some knowledge of the new learning now coming from Italy. I was acquainted with the tongue but the letters were all strung together like pearls on a string and

I could not make any sense. Only the letters 'IAK' stirred a chord in my memory but they were not enough.

I was finished by early evening and Stillington rejoined me in the chamber. He carefully examined both manuscripts, pronounced himself happy and let me go. He repeated his assurances that if he discovered what the manuscript contained he would send for me immediately. I reciprocated, though we were both lying. He did not even bother to ask me the name of my house or the street in which I resided. Nevertheless, I was content and returned to my lodgings for a fitful night's sleep.

Three days later I arrived back in London. My journey would have been quicker but my departure from the city of Bath was hindered by the royal justices in Eyre. They had been holding their assizes in the town, empanelling juries, hearing cases and delivering judgments. By the time I left Bath the trials were complete. The justices went out to the great cross-roads outside the city gates where they sat on horseback while their officials hanged those found guilty of crimes ranging from murder to house breaking. The executioners were busy. The gallows at the cross-roads eight, great three-branched affairs were all used, the bodies dancing and twirling like something out of a nightmare, a dream from Hell. Around them neighbours or friends, as well as scores of idle onlookers, stood blocking the way, allowing no one to pass until each corpse hung silent. The leading justice, still in his purple robes, pronounced himself satisfied, raised himself in the stirrups and shouted that King Edward's justice had been done and seen to be done. The crowd broke up and we were allowed through. I only wished the King's justice could be tempered by more mercy, not only for those unfortunates hanged outside the gates of Bath but all the small people caught up in the mills of royal power.

Of course, Blanche was delighted to see me, shouting in mock annoyance, pretending to sulk. I was so pleased to see how much she had missed me. As usual, she had cleaned my chamber, re-stacking my books and parchments so I could find nothing. Yet, I was pleased and oh so happy. But, naturally, in every Eden there is a serpent and that same evening Rokesley turned up just as Blanche and I were going to retire, our bellies full of the richest meat and the best wine Bordeaux can grow. The evening had turned cold, a thick heavy mist rolling in from the river, creeping like the Angel of Death along the streets. I opened the door and Rokesley stepped through, cloaked and muffled in his hood. Even before he pulled the cowl back, I could sense his annoyance, his eyes and face drained of all humour.

'Where have you been?' he snapped. 'His Grace the Duke of Gloucester, not to mention His Eminence Bishop Renaldi, have been waiting for you!' He stepped closer. I noticed how pale his face was, the jaw clenched hard in fury. I drew back in amazement.

'Good God, man, I left the city. I have other business to attend to. I have a wife, friends. What am I supposed to do? Kick my heels like some lackey, not daring to leave my own house for fear you may want me? Sweet Christ!' I snarled. 'Who do you think you are, man? I am a citizen of this city, a physician, I can go where I want. I have received no instruction to stay!' Rokesley saw the annoyance in my eyes and so softened both his voice and manner.

'Luke! Luke!' He took me by the hand. 'I am sorry. I only carry orders from those above us.' He smiled. 'Whom did you go to see? Your brother?'

I shook my head, muttering about other business elsewhere. For some strange reason he looked relieved at that and delivered his message.

'Tomorrow morning, Luke, just after first light, His Grace the Duke of Gloucester, Bishop Renaldi and others will leave from the King's Steps at Westminster and travel to Chertsey. The abbot has already been warned and the tomb will be opened for us to inspect. You are to join us. Your skill and astute observation are regarded as most vital to this progress.' His smile faded. 'You will be there?'

I nodded and Rokesley took his leave,

slipping quietly through the door into the swirling mist outside.

The next morning the mist had lifted, giving way to a slow, heavy drizzle. The sky was overcast so it was difficult to determine first light and I was anxious not to miss my meeting. The bells of Westminster Abbey church were still pealing for Matins when I arrived at King's Steps. Even so, Gloucester and the others were waiting for me. Three great state barges were drawn up, the oarsmen hooded and cowled so they sat like ghostly monks. Gloucester was also taking men-at-arms, steel-clad figures in their black hauberks and helmets; the clash of their weapons sounding ominously along the deserted water side.

Renaldi, cursing in fluent Italian at the miseries of the English climate, was already in one barge. Gough greeted me, smirking as he announced that Gloucester was impatient to go. I looked down and saw his master, unrecognisable in his plain soldier's cloak, the hood half-pulled across his red hair. I shrugged, not bothering to give an excuse, and clambered in after Gough. Orders rang out, one by one the barges were pushed away, the upraised oars lowered, manoeuvring the crafts into mid-stream and soon they were rising and falling as rhythmically as any drum beat, slicing the water as we headed up stream. The journey was completed in an hour. Hardly a word spoken except for the loud, clear commands given by the barge masters who, under Gloucester's insistence, were to keep the barges together.

The Duke himself did not even acknowledge my presence until we disembarked and were on the main pathway leading to the abbey gates.

'Master Physician,' he called over, 'it is good to see you. We had been waiting for you. After all, this is your idea.'

'Your Grace,' I explained tentatively, 'I am the King's loyal subject but there is more to my life, as you can appreciate, than what the King wants.'

Surprisingly, Gloucester grinned mischievously, clapped me on the shoulder and strode ahead, Gough trailing behind him. The abbey gates swung open and the

Abbot, followed by the Prior and other officers of the abbey, came out to greet us. There were the usual official civilities. I recognised the Abbot and went towards him. I was surprised to see the angry look he threw me before turning his back as a sign that I, for one, was not welcome. All I could do was shrug and follow the rest of the party into the abbey church. Gloucester's men-at-arms stood on guard outside whilst more stood in the nave and before the high altar, their swords drawn, not caring about the peace and security they were violating.

The Lady Altar on the left side of the abbey church was completely sealed off by huge, wooden screens, barriers which blocked all view or access into the chapel except the small opening we had to squeeze through. Gloucester led us in. The Lady Chapel was completely transformed, huge cresset torches had been lit and placed on the wall and the ground was covered with rubble. The Prior and six lay brothers joined us. He announced how the Abbot objected to the peace of his monastery being disturbed, the Lady

Chapel being turned into a mason's pit and, with a wave of his hand, the tomb of the late King Henry opened. Nevertheless, the monks realised they had to obey the express command of the King. So, it was best if the matter was finished as quickly as possible. Gough sniggered. Gloucester, leaning against the pillar, nonchalantly scraped the mud from the hem of his cloak whilst Renaldi, hands clasped and head bowed, patiently heard the Prior out. The envoy thanked the Prior with some diplomatic phrases but Gloucester brusquely interrupted.

'Father, may I have a torch?' The Prior handed him one from its wall socket and Gloucester walked over to the late King's tomb, gesturing at me to follow. The paving stones in front of the tomb had been raised. A mine shaft, similar to those dug under the walls of a besieged castle, had been dug, deep and broad enough to take two men standing shoulder to shoulder. Gloucester knelt and lowered the torch and I saw how the tunnel went under the stone sarcophagus.

'Two of your lay brothers please,

Father!' Gloucester ordered. The two fellows shuffled forward, their reluctance obvious in their white, strained faces but they had no choice. At Gloucester's bidding they lowered themselves into the tunnel, crawling under the sarcophagus. One eventually crept back, his face grimed with dirt.

'Your Grace,' he whispered hoarsely, 'the tomb is now open. The coffin is made of heavy wood. We can turn it round and push it to here where it will have to be lifted with ropes.'

Gloucester had no difficulty in understanding the man's rustic accent.

'Good!' he murmured. 'Get on with it!'

The man disappeared back into the tunnel. We heard a scraping noise and murmured groans of protest which echoed through the eerie silence of that darkened Lady Chapel. We all stood frozen like statues. Gloucester, one foot on a pile of rubble, watched the tunnel opening like a cat waiting for some mouse to reappear. Renaldi seemed over-awed. The Prior shocked by what he considered to be a blasphemy and a sacrilege whilst his servants stood like frightened children. One of the lay brothers re-emerged from the tunnel, coughing and spluttering, his back to us as he pulled and heaved at a mud-spattered, faded, wooden casket. At long last the coffin lay open to view at the bottom of the pit. Gloucester ordered the lay brothers out, ropes were lowered, fastened securely beneath the base of the coffin and, under Gloucester's commands, carefully raised and placed on the side of the pit. More orders and the coffin was moved until it lay full in front of the Lady Altar. The mud was cleared off the lid and Gloucester turned to the Prior.

'Father, I thank you for your help. You and your assistants may now go.'

The Prior walked across until his face was only a few inches from that of Gloucester. My heart warmed to see the man's courage.

'Your Grace,' he announced solemnly. 'This is a holy place. This tomb is a sacred memorial. I am the Abbot's chief officer in this abbey. The lay brothers, yes,' he shrugged. 'They can wait outside but I know my rights and I will stay.' Gloucester looked away, biting his lip, his hand falling to toy with the handle of his dagger. I thought he was going to refuse but, there again, that dazzling smile as if he not only agreed with the Prior but welcomed the suggestion.

'You are most correct, Father,' he answered. 'I would appreciate it if you stayed.'

Once the lay brothers had left, we gathered in a circle around the coffin. Gloucester gave both myself and Gough a knife which we ran under the mud-caked rim of the coffin, loosening its clasps. As we worked, I recollected that Henry had been buried for almost seven years. Corruption would be complete so there would be no putrid smell or foul odours. Yet I swear to this, and we all felt the same: as the lid was loosened, we caught a fragrance, sweet and fresh, like that of roses crushed to distil an essence. I glanced up, Renaldi looked nervous, Rokesley, who had appeared from the shadows, was terrified. And Gloucester? God how the man changed. His face now

189

white, so tense I could see his facial muscles moving, his eyes almost glazed, fixed on what we were doing. He glanced sharply at me.

'What is it, man? Hurry up! Why do you delay?'

'The fragrance,' I whispered. 'Can you not smell it?' My voice was like a whisper but it seemed to boom around that empty chapel. I felt the sweat break out on my brow. A cold shiver along my spine. I think Gloucester would have derided me but on the other side of the coffin Gough, too, had stopped. His arrogant face now pale and frightened.

'I can smell it too,' he said hoarsely. 'Roses as in Ashby's garden.'

I looked across quickly. Why had Gough remembered that?

'Hurry up!' Gloucester snarled.

We continued, my knife slipping along the rim, freeing the clasps then along the base whilst Gough worked at the top. Not a difficult task. The coffin was made of pine wood, stained with some substance which had turned the wood almost black but kept it well preserved. At last the lid was loose, the smell of roses now gone. Gloucester stepped back, Gough with him, almost happy to be away. Renaldi, however, came closer.

'Master Luke,' he urged, 'lift the lid!'

I slid it to the floor, revealing a thick, heavy, gauze-like material. It reminded me of white froth upon water. Once it had been cloth but the passage of time had corrupted it. I cleared this away, revealing the faded, red ermine-lined edge of the coffin. At first I panicked. Was there a body here? Then in one sweep I cleared the remnants of the gauze and revealed the corpse. I admit, Stephen, I just knelt and stared, although all around me I could hear the gasps of my companions. Henry the Sixth's body lay dressed in a monk's habit and cowl. The long thin face had the heavy grey pallor of death, the cheeks were quite sunken and the hands across his chest so thin the skin seemed only to veil the long bones. Nevertheless, the corpse looked as if it had been buried no more than a week. The face was perfectly recognisable, the heavy jaw, the high cheek bones, the steel grey hair peeping from beneath the hood.

'Uncorrupted,' Renaldi whispered. 'The body has not been corrupted!'

He gazed wildly around.

'Sirs, we are in the presence of something miraculous!'

Gloucester and Gough stepped back, their faces astonished, frightened, more wary of this old man's dead body than a charging warrior. The Prior just knelt down, his hands joined in prayer. I could not see Rokesley but heard his footsteps as he walked back into the darkness. All I could do was kneel and stare.

Gloucester, now unwilling to come closer, seemed wary of the task but, at Renaldi's insistence, I exclaimed the corpse, gently, carefully, as if I was holding a new-born babe. The skin was cold and clammy but Renaldi was right. It had not decomposed, no corruption had set in. With the Legate's help I pushed the King's death garb this way and that, examining the vein-rimmed legs, arms and chest of the dead monarch. Of course, I am a physician. The dead do not concern me. I have no fears of ghosts. No

192

repugnance of handling the soul's husk. I could see no marks of violence. There were some blueish marks on the thin rib cage but nothing significant. We turned the body over. Renaldi working like a common labourer as if the miracle had removed both his pretensions as well as his fear of the dead. Beside us the Prior softly chanted a psalm. Again, no marks of violence on the spine but the back of the skull was a different matter. In the centre, just above the neck, a crack like that of an egg. I laid the corpse face down, told Renaldi to bring me a candle and examined the blackened wound. Two things I noted. First, the dead king had an unusually thin skull, albeit the passage of time in the grave would have only heightened the effect of this. Secondly, the gash had been caused by some blunt instrument once, twice, as if delivered in some form of murderous frenzy. I looked at the position of the death wound, got up and walked behind the praying Prior.

'Father,' I said. 'Please, I beg you, kneel up straight.' The man did so. I grasped a small candlestick and swung it, pretending to strike him in the same place as the dead King's body but it was impossible. I put the candlestick down but the Prior suddenly bowed his head and I realised how the late King Henry had been killed. He had been at his prayers, head bowed when the assailant struck. But why, I wondered, strike him with the handle of a dagger? Why not just drive the blade deep into his back? I stood but could think of no solution. Gloucester was now stirring himself, joined by Gough and Rokesley.

'You have made your examination, Physician?' the Duke snapped.

'Yes, Your Grace. The late King was murdered by a blow to the base of his skull. By whom I do not know.'

'But could a dagger hilt cause such injury?' Rokesley asked. His face still drawn, eyes staring. I looked at him.

'Yes. Yes. The late King's skull was thin, abnormally so for such a man.'

'I agree with the physician,' Renaldi interjected. 'The late King was murdered but, more importantly, proof that his body has not corrupted is proof of his

194

sanctity. God's work surely?'

'Do you agree, Luke?' Rokesley asked. 'Have we witnessed a miracle?'

'Perhaps so,' I said. 'But the preservation of a corpse could be due to other matters more relevant to the world of nature than the intervention of God's good grace. It is possible for a body, especially that of an ascetic like Henry the Sixth, to be so completely sealed in a casket as to slow down or even stop the onset of corruption.

'I must protest!' Renaldi interrupted again. 'What we have witnessed is a miracle and I shall report it as such to His Holiness in Rome.'

'I mean no disrespect,' Gloucester snapped. 'You can tell it to Saint Peter himself. Such matters do not concern us.'

He turned and ordered Gough to stay and supervise the body being placed back in the coffin and resealed in its tomb. He bowed to the Prior, murmured the barest of thanks and swept out of the church, his retainers falling in behind him as we returned to the barge. The journey back was a silent one. Renaldi tried to engage me in conversation but I was too absorbed in what I had seen. Was it a miracle or an accident of nature? There was something else I had seen or heard which nagged at my memory; like a tune played on a viol, heard and forgotten, but the memory still strains to recapture it.

I thought of Gough and how I had observed, for the first time, that he was missing the top half of three fingers on his right hand. I had not noticed it before as the fellow constantly wears gloves. I knew it should mean something but I was too tired to concentrate. Instead, I went back to Ashby's manuscript. It still puzzled me, the word 'IAK' — where had I seen it before? And another word — 'SUHTXI' at the beginning. I was still chasing, teasing the problem when we disembarked at Westminster.

Renaldi invited me to sup within his own chambers but I graciously refused. Gloucester watched my play-acting, smirked and stalked off, shouting for his retainers to follow him. I went back, up the deserted, rain-drenched streets to my own house, tired yet a little pleased.

Perhaps the exhumation of the late King Henry's body might mean the end of the affair. Renaldi had enough evidence. Perhaps he would now leave me in peace. I idly considered quitting the court, for this business had wearied me. I am tired of the intrigue, the constant smell and threat of danger. I thought of the peace of Chertsey Abbey. Why had the abbot been so hostile? I remembered the conversation of one of Richard's servants as we clambered in the barge, something about the abbot still being resentful over his abbey being searched. What does that mean?

I stopped outside my house, surprised to see the shutters at the windows still open. Inside, I could see lights, the flaring flame of a candle and heard Blanche's soft singing. I stood watching the serenity of the scene and jumped as I felt my hand stroked. I looked, a young lad stood there, eyes gleaming in his dirty face.

'You are the physician?'

I nodded. The lad screwed up his eyes.

'The day after tomorrow,' he intoned, 'Master Trollope will meet you at noon in the tavern known as the 'Joy of Jerusalem' in Southwark.'

He opened his eyes and stretched out an even dirtier hand.

I pressed some coins into it and he ran off like the wind before I could question him.

So, brother, more yet. I put a brave face on it and went in to be teased by Blanche. Now it is night and I sit and write this letter to you. God save us both.

Written on the Feast of St. Andrew 1477.

Letter 6

Luke Chichele to his brother Stephen, monk in Aylesford Priory. Health and greetings.

The day after I despatched my last letter, I stayed with Blanche who questioned me like some lawyer on where I had been and what I had seen. She screwed up her pretty face in concentration as she listened to my replies. Strange, perhaps beneath it all I am a troubadour as romantic as any from Provence. When I married Blanche, I believed she was my Damoiselle, my princess. We men make such mistakes. Why do we accept the logic that a pretty face and a luscious body has no brain? Blanche constantly surprises me. She would not let me go but interrogated me as carefully as any serjeant-at-law in the Courts of Common Pleas.

At first, my answers were short and blunt but eventually I told her the whole story about my journey to Bath and the meeting with Stillington. She sat on a stool like some wise old woman, nodding her head, asking to repeat this phrase or that before demanding to see the document I had copied. In her youth Blanche had her own horn book and teachers who had instructed her in History, Latin and French but she confessed that, despite her learning, the memorandum meant as little to her as it did to me. I told her about the word 'IAK' and, taking her over to the window, copied it on the damp glass. I also scrawled the word 'SUHTXI.' Blanche stared at them but could make no sense of it.

'This document, Luke,' she concluded in exasperation, 'is the root of all the mystery. Ashby wrote it in some secret cipher to satisfy his conscience about the confidences given under the seal of confession.' She stared at me. 'Once you know it, Luke, you could be in greater danger.'

Of course, I did not tell her about Trollope's puzzling message. I thought the lawyer had been killed, taken his own life, or abjured the realm and fled beyond the seas. So why the meeting? The following morning I crept quietly out of the house. Watkins the boatman took me across the choppy river to Southwark. He could see I was withdrawn and tense so he regaled me with a string of stories about fornicating friars and lustful nuns. Perhaps he thought I was frightened of the river for the water rose and fell and the clinging cold mist was as freezing as a stepmother's breath. I am glad you were not with me, Stephen. Your face would have blushed as red as a beacon at Watkins' picture of your cloistered brethren. We landed at the fish wharf in Southwark. Despite the cold I pushed my cloak back over my shoulders, allowing all comers to see the knife and dagger strapped to my belt for Southwark is a veritable hell-hole. The prostitutes flock here as thick as starlings on a freshly ploughed field. Every dirty corner and filthy alleyway has its own small gang of rifflers eager to strike, even in daylight, at the unsuspecting. Thin, ragged children scurried around like mice in a hay rick, shouting and screaming, dashing in and out of the small houses, even swinging on the ale-stakes pushed under the eaves of the shabby inns. The air stank with a mixture of pungent smells from the open sewers which run rank and foul, as well as from the tanners, skinners and brick burners who ply their trade in a host of small rooms and wooden sheds.

Every second house seems to be a tavern and I had some difficulty finding 'The Joy of Jerusalem' which stood on a corner of a darkened alleyway where mangy, thin-ribbed cats angrily fought over heaps of rubbish. Inside, however, the tavern was surprisingly clean. A long, dark room, the windows small and affording very little light, ideal for any man hiding from the law. Two gamblers sat dicing in a corner and did not even bother to look up when I came in. A large ale wife, her face round and cheerful, despite the blue scar which ploughed across her right cheek, came bustling up, shouting.

'What do you lack? What do you lack, sir?'

I settled myself on a stool behind a rickety table and looked around. Chickens were roosting on the edge of the beer barrel. I decided I did not wish my ale to be spiced with their dung so I paid heavily for an unstoppered flagon of wine.

'Claret, the best the house has?' I muttered.

The ale wife grinned at me as if I was her long lost son and quickly returned with her cleanest cup and a bottle still sealed. She left me alone and I stayed, sitting there sipping slowly from the cup. I did not wish to get drunk. I heard the bells of a distant church chiming the mid-day Angelus but still no sign of Trollope. People came and went but only the gamblers stayed and an old crone who became as drunk as a blind singer's dog. The afternoon drew on. I became restive, heavy-eyed as the wine and the cloying warmth of the tavern had their effect. I stood up, preparing to go, believing I had come on a fool's errand when the gamblers also rose and ambled towards me. My hand went to my knife but, now I faced them, I sensed they were not the usual visitors to such a place. Oh, they were dressed shabbily enough. A man can hide his face, let his beard grow, tousle his hair and wear untidy, ill-fitting clothes but he is always betrayed by his hands. I noticed how the fingers of both men were clean and soft, the nails carefully pared. I shrugged and sat down. They pulled over stools and sat opposite me, smiling as if they were old friends. One was tall, thin, his face white and gaunt under a bush of shocking red hair. The other was smaller, fat and bald, and as cheerful looking as Friar Tuck from some story of Robin of the green wood. They were dressed in tattered patched robes which were clasped at the neck but, as they sat down, both of them moved a little to accommodate the long daggers concealed underneath. One of them summoned the ale wife.

'Two cups!' he demanded.

Once she had brought them, the man, without any bidding, refilled mine and theirs to the brim. The balding one toasted me, his light, grey eyes smiling as he sipped gratefully from the cup.

'I hope you enjoy my wine,' I began sarcastically. 'I was keeping it for a friend.'

'Monsieur Trollope?' the stout man queried.

I nodded.

'Unfortunately,' the fellow continued and I caught the strong trace of an accent. 'Unfortunately, Monsieur Trollope cannot meet you.' He joined his hands together as if in prayer. 'You see, Monsieur Chichele, Trollope is dead.'

He leaned back, his eyes wide and watched as my hand went under my own cloak for the dagger I kept there. His elder companion now moved closer and touched me gently on the arm.

'No, Monsieur, we are not responsible and we mean you no harm. We simply wish to ask you some questions. Let us introduce ourselves. I am Jean Lavalle and this,' he turned to his short, balding companion, 'is Pierre Roche.'

I rested my back against the wall and sighed. So Trollope was dead. My suspicions were correct.

'You kept me waiting,' I said.

'We had to make sure, Monsieur, you did not bring others with you.'

'Have you been following me?' I asked.

Lavalle shook his head.

'No. But we know someone has been watching you. We have seen him outside and, undoubtedly, he will be waiting when you leave. A short, fair-haired man. I doubt if you would know him, some villain from the city who is keeping you under observation.' Lavalle smiled. 'But you are safe with us.' He looked around the tavern. 'We know this place well and there are other entrances and doors whereby you can leave. But first, our questions.'

'Why should I answer them?' I asked. Somehow I did not feel alarmed or threatened. Both men had taken every care to allay my fears and I knew, deep within my soul, that they posed no threat. I scrutinised them carefully.

'Let me consider,' I said, 'who you are. You are both French yet you know the city well. I suspect you are merchants but also servants of Louis the Eleventh of

France. Am I correct?'

The smaller one, Roche, grinned.

'Almost,' he said. 'Monsieur Lavalle here is a merchant but I am chief clerk in the retinue of the French envoy to the court of your master, King Edward the Fourth of England.' His face became serious. 'Look, Monsieur, we know the commission you have been given. We know you have been attacked and two of your colleagues murdered. Finally, we suspect you hold a clue to some great mystery which affects Edward of England.'

'So why should I act the traitor,' I replied, 'and tell you business which is not yours to know?'

Lavalle shrugged and called for another flagon of wine. He waited until the ale wife had bustled away.

'You are correct,' he answered. 'You need not tell us. We would have preferred to ask George, Duke of Clarence but,' he refilled my cup, 'as you know, Clarence has been taken. He is lodged in the Tower and we do not think he will leave it alive.'

'So, Clarence was a traitor,' I jibed.

'Yes,' Roche replied slowly. 'Clarence was a traitor. Let us be honest. My master, Louis of France, fears Edward of England. He does not want to see English bowmen burning our cities again. Edward's brother, George of Clarence, has always been a traitor. For a while he fought with the Lancastrians against his own family and, when their star fell, he turned to our master.' Roche smiled and drew strange designs on the wine-soaked table. 'Clarence loves his brother Edward but hates and detests Edward's wife. He sees her as a commoner, a treacherous witch, who beguiled his brother with her beautiful face and diabolical arts. Clarence hoped to secure a marriage alliance with some foreign princess and use any dowry to raise troops against his brother. Of course, my master agreed.' Roche paused and shrugged. 'But Clarence is stupid, he talks too much. My master, King Louis, realised it would come to nothing so he betrayed Clarence to Edward. After all, in this busy world of politics, a Prince cannot afford to have friends.'

I stared down at the table. Roche was speaking the truth. Louis the Fourth the Spider King, had his web of spies wrapped round every court in Christendom. He trusts no one. You may have heard the rumours, even in your monastery, Stephen, how Louis protects himself against assassination by buying every holy relic on sale in the market place. He hides in his castle behind ranks of archers, revolving watch towers and iron fences. He has a taster for everything he eats and drinks as well as his own special orchard where he hangs those who have tried to poison him. He takes guests out to view the decaying fruit like any other man surveys his garden. Louis would do anything to embarrass Edward of England and Clarence was his natural foil.

'What are you thinking, Monsieur?' Roche broke my reverie.

'As you say, Monsieur,' I replied, 'in this vale of tears, a Prince can have no friends. But why should Louis be interested in my commission?'

I moved the cup away from me.

'Oh, I can see how the canonisation of Henry of England would seriously embarrass the House of York. King Louis would crow with delight. But there is more is there not? Something else?'

Lavalle, who had been quietly supping from his own cup, nodded vigorously.

'Of course, Monsieur. Clarence told our master how Henry of England knew something dreadful about the House of York. His priest, Ashby, had this secret. Clarence promised to sell it to our master and Trollope was his intermediary. Ashby, however, seemed most reluctant to betray his secret then, of course, he died. Now Trollope is dead, garrotted, trussed up like some chicken. His body now lies decaying in his chamber above a shop in Catte Street.' He smiled sourly at me. 'Oh, yes, he has been dead for some time. His body lies beneath the floor boards, the garrotte string still around his throat. I suppose some official will discover the corpse when it begins to smell. We ransacked his chamber but found nothing so, we came to you.'

'Again, I ask,' I interrupted. 'Why

should I help you? I am the King's loyal subject. How do I know who you claim to be? You may be agents of His Grace, the Duke of Gloucester, even of King Edward himself.'

Lavalle dug into his purse and brought out a small script. Its message was short and terse: 'Jean Lavalle is a loyal subject, an officer of the King of France', and the purple wax blob bore the secret seal of Louis the Eleventh. I handed it back.

'So, I know who you are. But why should I help you?'

Roche leaned over the table, using his fat, stubby fingers to emphasise his sentences.

'First, unlike Clarence or Trollope, we know you are not interested in power or wealth but the truth. Secondly, although it makes no difference to us, we believe you know Henry of England was a holy man, brutally murdered. You opened his tomb at Chertsey and found proof of that. Thirdly, you are a man without powerful friends.' He raised a hand to fend off any protest. 'Believe me, Monsieur, no one at the English Court will help you. Fourthly, we know that those above you do not trust you. You are being watched. Your life is in as great a danger as Ashby's or Trollope's and could be snuffed out,' he snapped his fingers, 'like that, in some dark alleyway or dingy street! Even worse, Monsieur, like Clarence you may find yourself facing allegations of treason. I respect you, Monsieur, and I do not mean to frighten you, Ashby and Trollope were solitary men but you have a beautiful young wife.' He saw the alarm flare in my eyes and hurriedly continued, 'Don't you see, Luke, you are in danger and you cannot walk away from it? Your life means nothing to your Prince. I say this with no intended offence, no more than my life does to Louis of France. Finally, Monsieur, we have information which may help you. All we ask is that you take this information and, if the worst should happen,' he shrugged, 'Louis of France will be more than eager to welcome a skilled and famous physician to his court.' He grinned. 'Of course, no Frenchman would refuse a welcome to your beautiful lady wife.'

I stared at both the Frenchmen and wildly wondered what to do. I admired the Frenchman's cleverness. He was not asking me to betray the King. Indeed, I would not. All he was offering was information which might help me in my commission and I, a faithful officer of the King, had every duty to take it. I relaxed and leaned across the table.

'Monsieur Roche, I cannot tell you what is secret and privy to the King but I will listen to you.'

Both men studied me carefully and glanced at each other. Lavalle nodded and Roche leaned closer like a con- spirator.

'We do not know Clarence's secret,' he said. 'We suspect Clarence really knows nothing. However, we have another source.' He chewed his lip as he carefully considered his words. 'Henry the Sixth of England,' he continued, 'was married to a French princess, Margaret of Anjou. After the defeat of her armies at Barnet and Tewkesbury in 1471, she was held captive in England for a while.'

Roche paused and Lavalle took up the story.

'Our master ransomed Queen Margaret. She was a broken woman when he brought her back to France.' Lavalle stopped speaking and looked around the tavern to make sure there were no eavesdroppers.

'The Lady Margaret was desperate for money and, on one occasion, bargained with King Louis for gold in return for a dreadful secret. My master thought she was bluffing and was proved correct. The only thing he did learn was that Margaret, half demented with grief, said the dreadful secret was known by the good God, King Henry and the Lady Eleanor Butler. This is all our master could learn.' Lavalle smilingly leaned back and extended his hands. 'Who,' he asked, 'is the Lady Eleanor Butler? And what did she know?'

Butler? The name meant nothing to me. What had she to do with this great mystery? No lady at court bore that name nor was she ever mentioned in its tittle-tattle. I shook my head.

'Messieurs, I cannot help you. The name means nothing to me. I can assist you no further.'

Both men smiled but then Lavalle suddenly seized me by the wrist.

'Monsieur, one day you will know and, if you wish, we will be of help.'

He looked towards the door and I followed his gaze. It was early afternoon and it was already turning dark.

'I should go,' I murmured.

'Not that way!' Roche rose and called for the ale wife.

She bustled across, Roche whispered to her and dropped coins into her calloused hand. She smiled and beckoned at us, leading us over to a far corner of the tavern. She plucked a key from her belt and unlocked a side entrance which led into an alleyway. Lavalle and Roche stepped through with me behind them. They both stood there, hoods up over their heads, cloaks tight around them. Lavalle moved forward, hand extended to bid me 'adieu' and the arrow bolt took him full in the mouth. All I heard was the whirr, like that of a bird swooping for the kill, and caught something black as it skimmed past my eye. The poor Frenchman, however, had no such chance. The jagged crossbow bolt turned his face into a mask of blood and he crashed wordlessly to the ground. Roche, pulling me by the cloak, shoved and pushed me down the alleyway.

'Run!' he whispered hoarsely.

We did, even as a second crossbow bolt smashed on to the cobbles between us. Roche glanced back at his fallen comrade. He looked pleadingly at me.

'I cannot leave him,' he whispered.

God knows I reasoned with him but Roche drew his dagger and, keeping to the alley wall, edged back to where Lavalle lay face down in an ever growing puddle of blood. Turning the body over, Roche cut the wallet from the dead man's belt and hurried back to join me. I was pressed against the wall so the hidden marksman would not surprise us and Roche had nearly reached me when, again, I heard that horrid whirring. Roche leaned towards me like a swimmer, his hands out, eyes staring, his mouth opening and closing, gasping for air. He stumbled against the wall, looked up pitifully at me, whispered, 'Jesu, mercy!' and dropped like a bundle of rags; the cross bow bolt with its iron jagged point was embedded firmly between his shoulder blades. This time I did not wait but fled. Again I heard the smack of a crossbow quarrel hitting the wall; and, despite my panic, I realised there must be two, not one assassin. Perhaps it was the darkness, or maybe they did not wish to kill me but I escaped from that death-strewn alleyway and joined the beggars, pimps and whores now thronging the streets of Southwark. I was racked by constant terror and stayed with the crowd though I knew the assassin or his accomplice could sidle up and slip a dagger between my ribs.

God be thanked, I reached the river side safely. Watkins the boatman, was waiting and I tumbled gratefully into his wherry. I shouted he should row as fast as he could, hastily pressing a silver coin into his dirty hand.

'Pull man! Pull!' I yelled.

He needed no second bidding and, as his small boat drew away from the bank, I looked back through the gathering darkness but neither the fading daylight nor the huge spluttering tar torches on the river bank revealed any sign of a pursuer. For perhaps the only time in his life Watkins kept his mouth shut. He pulled lustfully at the oars, watching me closely under his heavy-lidded eyes, curious at my sheet-white face, clammy skin and obvious look of terror. By the time we reached the far bank I had regained some of my composure but I was unwilling to go home. Blanche would know there was something wrong and I did not wish to alarm her. Instead, I went to a nearby tavern and wolfed down a dish of rancid dry meat, masking the taste with mouthfuls of thick, heavy claret. I felt like some hungry dog, fear whetting my appetite, whilst I ate I kept looking up, staring around the gloomy tavern room, looking suspiciously at anyone who dared even catch my eye.

By the time I had finished my meal, anger had replaced my fear; fury at the way I, a loyal subject of the King, a respected doctor, was being hunted like some animal along the filthy alleyways of London. I made a resolve. I would find out who Eleanor Butler was and return home. The following morning I would demand an audience with the Queen, tell her everything that had happened and ask to be relieved of this commission. I left the tavern and, begging a ride from a carter, made my way up into the palace of Westminster. I will not bore you with the details, Stephen. I have friends, clerks from the Court of Common Pleas and in the Exchequer. They were about to finish the business of the day, rolling up their documents, clearing the abacus, locking coffers and chests but I seized one, Thomas Tunstall, and begged for his help. One of the virtues of being a physician is being indispensable. I had given Tunstall physic after an attack of colic and not charged him a fee. I brusquely reminded him of this favour and, weary-eyed, he told me to wait. Armed with a candle and quietly mouthing his protests, he went to search amongst the Calendar of Land

Inquisitions for the name of Eleanor Butler. A good hour passed before he returned to the musty, dark chamber.

'Your Lady Eleanor,' he muttered, 'was the daughter of John Talbot, first Earl of Shrewsbury, she married Thomas Butler, knight. After he died, her manors were seized by the late King Henry the Sixth but then restored by our present lord King.'

'Is that all?' I asked.

Tunstall shrugged.

'What more is there? She died suddenly in 1468.'

'Nothing else?'

Tunstall shook his head.

'Nothing remarkable. A petty land-owner of no real importance, that is all.'

I left Tunstall in his dark warren of chambers in Westminster Palace. I was still nervous after the murderous assault and whispered a quiet prayer for the repose of the souls of the two Frenchmen who must have died instantly. I knew enough about abarlests to realise that and did not want the attack repeated. Outside Westminster I went to where the empty stalls were and hired two burly porters, their work now finished, to escort me back to my own chambers. Coins exchanged hands and, like two faithful mastiffs, they padded quietly in front of me, one of them carrying a torch, until I reached my house and dismissed them.

I paused to smooth my hair and make sure my garments bore no traces of the violence I had been through. It was dark, Blanche had placed candles in the windows, the shutters being still drawn back. I heard the faint singing and drew closer to the window, just to catch a glimpse of her beautiful serenity. I love watching her and I am glad I did. In that moment Ashby's riddle was solved, that is why I am telling you about it now, Stephen. Leaving the good wine to last to show that all is not ill news. Remember, earlier in the day I had scrawled on the window pane Ashby's strange terms 'IAK' and 'SUHTXI?' Now I caught their reflection. The right way round 'IAK' is really 'KAI' the Greek word for 'and'; 'SUHTXI,' of course is 'IXTHUS,' the Greek for 'Christ'. I stared in disbelief before breaking into peals of laughter, causing Blanche to come running to the door, shouting at me for making a disturbance for all the neighbours to hear. I told her and she seemed pleased, so pleased her sharp eyes did not notice my own fears.

Finally, Blanche told me a messenger had come from Aylesford bringing a parcel from you. Is it a present, dear brother? He would not hand it to Blanche but said he would return tomorrow evening for he had been instructed to give it to me personally. I look forward to that. God keep you, Stephen. December 1477.

Letter 7

Luke, physician, to Brother Stephen, monk of Aylesford Priory.

So strange how worlds can be shattered by the stopping of a heart. Two hearts have ceased beating and my happy world has crashed like some house whose foundations have been shaken loose. I write this letter with difficulty and see it as a confession, a last will and testament, an expression of justice. I would love to scream, write the filthiest epithets, curse God and every man who calls himself a prince and damn the whores they marry but, let my story unfold. Blanche is dead. You know that. Surely, you have seen her? No, I must not say that. Let me explain, Blanche is dead. Cold and lifeless, her body buried under a transept off the nave in our parish church. Already the chantry priests sing Masses for her soul but, if there is a paradise and a good God, like you, she will have no need of them.

Blanche has died. Again a lie. Blanche was murdered.

The day after I wrote to you last, the feast of the Virgin, no I get confused, the morning after the feast, Blanche had gone into the garden. God knows why. Perhaps to inspect the soil or just to leave scraps out for the birds, for the weather was cold and she had great pity for them freezing on the branches. She went out in my old robe, the hood pulled over her head for there was a sudden flurry of snow. The sky was full of it, great dark clouds gathering over the city as if they were to mourn what was about to happen. Blanche must have knelt down, crouching to see something closer, when a crossbow bolt hit her full in the back. Its jagged barb smashed skin, bone and gouged a hole for her life blood to ebb out.

Strange, I was here in my own chamber, still locked in the stupidity which brought it all about, fearful of what I had discovered for I had broken Ashby's cipher. All I had to do was copy out the manuscript again, only this time turning the letters round. I used a lexicon, a

Greek book I had bought in Salerno when I studied the manuscripts of Hippocrates and Galen. Once the words were written out in their proper form according to the lexicon, I simply divided one word from another. God forgive me, I digress. What matters now if I know secrets which can rock thrones? As I said, I was in my chamber when the maid came bustling in, hysterical and screaming.

'My lady! My lady!'

I jumped up, my chair falling over, pushed her aside and ran into the garden. Blanche lay face down in the snow, her face quite serene, her eyes half-open, a thin streak of blood still seeping out of the corner of her mouth and, in her back, the great, jagged, death-bearing barb. Oh, I howled like a dog, frantic that with all my skill, learning and physic, I was helpless and could do nothing. One of the apprentices went for a friend, a colleague, an old physician called Theodore who lived nearby. He gave me a potion which calmed the rage seething in my heart and stopped my mouth spewing out filthy epithets at whoever came near me.

I stayed in a deep sleep for almost a day whilst men and women, no more than strangers, showed me more kindness than I had met in my life. Theodore took care of Blanche. He gently removed the barb, dressing her body for burial, sending messages to the priests, paying church fees, buying a coffin, candles, tapers all the mummery and frippery we buy to hide from ourselves the dreadful fact of death. Two days later Blanche was buried and I watched as if in some dreadful nightmare. I hoped I would pinch myself and awake to find Blanche beside me, calm, serene and ready to kiss the pain and hurt away. But Blanche was gone. The coffin lowered beneath the flagstone in the church, the Masses said, the incense burnt, the chanting priests silent. Nothing left but a terrible loneliness and the flowering of a dark foulness in my own soul. A rare mixture. A growth of guilt, anger, rage and the lust for vengeance. It kept me sane. If it had not been for that, I would have slipped quietly over the edge of the deep bottomless pit of brooding melancholy.

I called the sheriff and established how Blanche had died. The assassin, the same bastard who killed the Frenchmen, must have been waiting, high in a room in an adjoining house. Nothing much, a collection of chambers for clerks and scriveners who work in the Chancery or Exchequer at Westminster. Of course, nobody saw anything. Oh, a stranger had been seen, dressed in deep Lincoln green, his face hooded. Yes, he may have carried a cross bow but that was all. I knew one thing. Blanche had died in my stead. The murderer, some professional assassin, had been given my description. Perhaps he waited for me in the street and, impatient at the way I had closeted myself in my own chamber poring over Ashby's manuscript, took the decision to kill me whenever the opportunity presented itself.

Oh, the Court was distressed. Those royal hypocrites sent messages of condolence, gifts, tokens of appreciation. They are still piled in a chamber beyond the buttery. Gough and Rokesley came to see me, skilful men with their closed faces. They did not dare to question me about the King's business but Blanche's death was no secret. Ashby was dead, Trollope was dead and, by all rights, so should I be. I let them stand in the hall and silently heard their messages out. Once they were gone I called the apprentices and scullion maids. I gave each a bag of coins and letters of recommendation to friends. I calmed their fears, telling them to go away, at least for a while, until I had recovered and the danger was past.

Grief can be a strange medicine. It can cloud the soul and fuddle the mind but it can also do the opposite. I felt cold yet calm; my soul lucid, my wits sharp, my mind cleared of all impedimenta and obstacles. Blanche was murdered. Her death caused by the task that I was involved in. The very affair she had so often railed against. Her words had been prophetic. Had she always sensed the danger? I cleared the desk in my own chamber and wrote down on sheets of parchment everything I knew. I also decided not to leave the house. I did not care if I lived or died but I did not want death to take me before my vengeance was complete. I sent gold and a message to Theodore and I hired a dozen of the city's most able-bodied rogues. Wolves in sheep's clothing, mercenaries, ex-soldiers who were paid to guard the approaches to my house and let no one in without my consent.

Oh, the usual messengers came. I fobbed them off but, finally, the one from you arrived. The package you sent but I did not open, so distracted was I by Blanche's death. I could not believe it, Stephen. If I could have cried, I would have done. If my heart was not broken it would have been. All I could do was place your message on the table and realise how quickly a life can be over. What had I done to deserve it? I took your message up, held it tight in my hand and it led me to the truth. My suspicions were aroused. I sent one of my messengers, the most intelligent of the mercenaries I had hired, with a sealed letter to Bishop Renaldi at Westminster. I ordered the man to speak to no one, to give my letter to no one save the Bishop himself. I asked Renaldi, as one human being to another, to answer my question but only inform me of the answer he got. His reply came within two days and I drew deeper into myself.

Now everything was clear. At last I knew why Cantrone had died as well as Ashby and Trollope. In a sense, my letters had caused their deaths. I also knew why Blanche had died and why the Abbot of Chertsey had been hostile towards me. Everything was so clear, like a ship breaking free of a mist so one can see every piece of sail, every carved, fretted bit of woodwork.

After that I concentrated on why these people had died. Yet, I knew the answer to that. Ashby's document had revealed the reason, so I moved on to the third part of the puzzle. Who were the murderers? And I went back to the beginning, recollecting everything which had happened to me since that first meeting of the commission in Baynards Castle. Day after day, stopping only to eat, drink and take a few hours sleep. My guards reported how strangers had been seen round my house but the sight of their naked swords prevented them drawing near. A royal writ came from Westminster ordering my presence there or I would incur the King's displeasure but I avoided the snare. I summoned the physician, Theodore and, at my request, he despatched a letter in reply, saying I was ill, some mysterious ailment. God forbid, it might be the plague. I knew the murderer at Westminster would doubt such a reply but not immediately. Another day passed and I had the truth. I sent an urgent note to Rokesley, begging him to attend upon me as early as possible that same evening. I told him I had some dreadful secret to impart, but only to him, he was not to tell Gough or any other.

The fellow arrived just after dark and my guards let him through. I had bought fresh pies from a baker in a nearby street and served the best wine my cellars held. Rokesley seemed surprised, nervous, but wine is one of the best medicines. It may cloud the mind but, as the psalmist says, it gladdens the heart. Once the meal was finished, I refilled his cup. Rokesley sipped appreciatively and turned his treacherous face towards me.

'Luke, we have missed you. What is this dreadful news you have to tell me?'

At that moment I became alive. The writer was correct when he said 'Vengeance is a dish best served cold' and I was to relish every bit. Rokesley jumped as a small door at the back of my house opened and slammed shut but I smiled reassuringly.

'Only the wind, Simon,' I said. 'There are more frightening things than that.'

'Such as?'

'Such as the truth, Simon.'

Rokesley leaned back in his chair, his hand falling on to his lap.

'Don't play games, Luke,' he said. 'Say what you have to.'

'Good,' I murmured. 'Then let me tell you the truth. We both serve on a royal commission to investigate the life and possible sanctity of the late King Henry the Sixth of England. Now we know,' I leaned forward, steepling my fingers, 'that King Henry was a saint, a pious man, probably the most venerated who has ever worn the crown of England.' I smiled. 'Perhaps a weak man, really a lamb married to a she-wolf who fought for him.'

'I know my history,' Rokesley interrupted.

'Well,' I continued, 'let us go to the end of it. In May 1471 King Henry's wife, Margaret, and the other Lancastrian generals were defeated at Barnet and Tewskesbury. King Henry, their nominal leader, was a prisoner in the Tower. On the night Edward returned to London, he resided in the Tower and that very same evening Henry was murdered. Most people believed King Edward was simply crushing the Lancastrian seed once and for all but, we both know, Simon, that King Edward had promised Henry his life. He had no desire to kill him.'

I was pleased to see Rokesley stir uncomfortably in his chair and lose some of his calm, arrogant poise.

'Gloucester!' he interrupted. 'Gloucester killed him!'

'Oh, no,' I said. 'Gloucester did not kill him nor did Clarence. You see, King

Henry was killed by a woman. You look startled, Simon?'

The fellow glared back. He was about to rise but I gestured him to sit down.

'Hear me out, Rokesley,' I said. 'On that May evening the Yorkist generals celebrated their victory, Edward and Clarence were probably drunk but Edward's Queen, Elizabeth Woodville, was not. She was frightened. Her husband had been in the west country fighting the she-wolf, Margaret of Anjou. Elizabeth knew that if Anjou had been victorious she would have been for the block or a nunnery. Elizabeth hated Henry, not only because he posed a threat to herself and her own children, there was something else. Henry knew some dreadful secret. So, on that evening, Elizabeth Woodville, armed with a dagger stolen from the Tower stores, went across to the Wakefield Tower. No guards were on duty. Perhaps they, too, were drunk or maybe the Queen had sent some faithful retainer, a man such as you, Rokesley, to tell them there was no need to guard an old witless man whose armies were now shattered.' I smiled sourly at him. 'Anyway, the Woodville woman went into Henry's chamber. God knows what happened then. Perhaps she baited him with his wife's terrible defeats and his own son's death. She may have repeated the rumours of how Queen Margaret's son was of bastard issue. King Henry, of course, would just sit there, watching with his great sad eyes, or scorned her, repeating what he knew about her and Edward.' I paused and took a sip from my own wine cup. 'Only God knows, but then Henry turned, knelt and continued with his prayers. Elizabeth Woodville could stand it no longer. She felt scorned, ridiculed and yet strangely frightened of this so-called witless old man. She clasped the dagger in her hand and moved closer, but Woodville was no soldier. She could not bear the sight of blood, the feel of the dagger sinking into the warm living flesh of a crowned, anointed King. Oh, no, she took the blade in her hand and, full of fury, dashed the hilt once, twice, perhaps a third time, bringing it down savagely on the back of the old King's head. Henry fell forward, perhaps turning in his death throes, though the wounds he had received were fatal. Woodville threw both sheath and dagger into the straw and fled.'

Rokesley, his hands on the table, leaned forward and shouted at me.

'You have no proof!' he said. 'You have no proof! How dare you malign the Queen!'

'That may be so,' I replied. 'But it is still the truth. You see, Rokesley, an assassin or a soldier would have used the blade but the Queen was squeamish and used the hilt. The Abbot at Chertsey has the dagger and remarked on the hairs and speckled blood stains he saw on the hilt. I suspect the Woodville woman told her husband and he sent the ever-loyal Gloucester to clear up the mess and take care of everything. He did, but overlooked the dagger, Cantrone found that and gave it to Chertsey Abbey.'

'You still have no proof that it was the Queen,' Rokesley interrupted. 'Nothing tangible.'

'Nothing except you,' I replied.

'What do you mean?'

'When we were at Chertsey exhuming the late King's body, you actually referred to the hilt of a dagger being used. Who told you that?'

'You did!' he snapped.

'No, I did not, Simon. At Chertsey I used a small candlestick. I made no reference to a dagger. You could have only learnt that from the Queen herself or, of course, from my letters.'

Rokesley attempted mock surprise.

'Oh, I'll come to that,' I said. 'But what I do know is that you thought the dagger was important. You knew I had seen it, that's why you murdered Cantrone and sent men to ransack Chertsey Abbey for it.'

Rokesley smiled and spread his hands.

'But the Queen did not tell me so how could I know?'

'As I have said, Woodville may have told you and, of course, in my letters so did I. However,' I held up my hand to stop any further interruption. 'The greatest proof that Woodville killed King Henry is what the old King knew, a dark

237

secret. When Clarence had been allied to him, Henry told this secret to John Ashby who, as we both know, was Clarence's chaplain and visited Henry in the Tower. At one of these meetings, Henry confessed. He told Ashby a strange story. How King Edward the Fourth could not be truly married to Elizabeth Woodville for he had been secretly affianced to another woman, Eleanor Butler, at the time of his marriage.' I relished the fear in Rokesley's face.

'You see, Rokesley, Canon Law is quite explicit on this. Our King Edward the Fourth could not have undertaken a valid marriage whilst affianced to the Butler woman. If that is true, then Elizabeth Woodville is not truly his wife. His two sons are bastards and have no legal claim to the throne of England. Lady Butler appealed and informed King Henry of this but he kept it a secret. Shortly afterwards Lady Eleanor died in rather mysterious circumstances. I suspect poison cannot be ruled out.' I stopped and watched Rokesley take a full gulp from the wine cup. 'We know our King is attracted to older women, particularly widows. Elizabeth Woodville should know, she was one.' I paused to sip from my goblet. 'Edward had dealings with Butler, gave her back certain manors, became infatuated with her but soon tired of it. I suppose he told Woodville and she never forgot. I suggest King Henry the Sixth slyly referred to it when she used to visit him in the Tower. Woodville must have been terrified when Clarence's men, also visited Henry. One of them, Ashby, actually heard the old King's confession. Of course Ashby realised,' I continued, 'the true importance of Henry's confession. He could not contain himself so he wrote it down in a secret cipher but then tore the manuscript in half. One piece he sent to Bishop Stillington of Bath and Wells, the other he hid in his own carp pond. Even so,' I continued, 'Ashby could not keep his mouth shut. He hinted at this dark secret both to Stillington and to Clarence. Stillington was dismissed from the Chancellorship and Clarence, as we know, has been marked down for destruction.'

'But how would the Queen know that King Henry had confessed to all this?' Rokesley interrupted.

'Only God knows,' I replied. 'As I have said, perhaps Henry intimated as much to her. Clarence hates her and maybe he teased her with the prospect of knowing some dreadful secret which, in fact, he did not. The Queen has a legion of spies. She would know the dreadful secret was out.'

Rokesley seemed to regain his composure.

'But the Queen welcomed our commission,' he commented, 'the investigation into King Henry the Sixth's life.'

'Oh, of course, she did,' I answered, 'admittedly Louis the Eleventh may have petitioned for it. We both know the French King. He would do anything to embarrass King Edward. Clarence, of course, hoped to dig up the old scandal which Ashby had hinted at but dare not divulge.'

I shrugged. 'We both know how a priest who breaks a seal of confession is immediately excommunicated and can only be absolved by the Pope himself.' I watched as Rokesley drank again from the deep, gold bowl, before continuing. 'The Queen sensed that villainy was afoot and realised Clarence might be searching again for the secret. After all, he had appointed two of his own people to the commission, Ashby and Trollope. So, in turn, she ensured that two men from her household, you and me, were also appointed.' I stopped and gazed into the darkness above Rokesley's head. I wished with all my soul that both you, dear Stephen, and Blanche had been present, in body as well as in spirit, to see justice done.

'Continue,' Rokesley slurred, his voice now quite thick.

'Ah,' I replied, 'that's when the killing began. You see, Ashby decided to confess that he knew King Henry was a saint. He wanted to tell us as much and so invited us to his house. You, of course, thought he was about to reveal the secret scandal. You ensured that you visited Ashby first. He took you out into the garden. He sat on a bench near his pond. You just tied the noose round his neck like the assassin you are and choked out his life. You knew I was coming so you tossed the corpse into the ice-cold carp pond. It would then appear that Ashby had been dead for hours but you forgot the cup of mulled wine Ashby had been drinking. I remembered that was still warm but Ashby's corpse was cold, not because he had been dead a long time but because he had been immersed in the frozen water.'

Rokesley shook his head.

'You have no proof of that,' he said.

'Oh, yes I do,' I replied. 'I know Burdett, Clarence's man, did not kill him. Trollope did not, indeed he died the same way. That left you or Gough. However, at Chertsey, I noticed how the fingers on Gough's right hand are severely damaged. As a physician I know that Gough may be a good dagger and swordsman but, with such malformed hands, he could never hold or pull a garrotte string.' I rose and, without asking, took Rokesley's cup and refilled it. 'The Queen,' I continued matter-of-factly, 'was now alarmed. Clarence, as impetuous and

242

foolish as ever, played into her hands. He was arrested and she used the crisis to have Trollope murdered and Ashby's death placed at Burdett's door.'

'If you know so much,' Rokesley loudly interrupted, 'why shouldn't the Queen have killed you?'

'She tried!' I shouted back angrily. 'I was attacked! I was followed. She did not want me dead. It would cast the finger of suspicion at her. Much better if I was frightened, made more pliable.' My voice broke with emotion. 'But when you both realised that I knew too much and could not be controlled, you sent the assassin. The murder of the Frenchmen was a mistake so the killer was sent back to complete the task. You gave him a description of me, my house and, above all, the robe I wore. He, God damn him, whoever he is, became tired of waiting. He took up his position in the house overlooking my garden. The day was dark, snow was falling. He let loose his murderous crossbow bolt and killed my wife by mistake, thinking it was me, not her in my robe.'

Rokesley looked dazed but still he tried to play the courtier.

'But if that is true, why should we want to kill you?'

'Because I was about to discover Ashby's secret.'

'But how could we know that? You told no one about that except Stillington and your wife?'

Rokesley raised his hand to his mouth as he realised the terrible mistake he had made.

'How do you know what I discussed with Stillington?' I replied quietly. 'Oh, I could tell you, Simon,' I continued, 'just as you knew about my conversation with Cantrone, as you did about the Abbey of Chertsey, the dagger and the record of miracles attributed to Henry the Sixth. You had Cantrone murdered and ransacked Chertsey. So, how did you know?' I felt the anger well within me. 'Because you intercepted the letters to my brother. You knew I wrote to him. How I told him everything that happened to me. You went to the Prior of Aylesford and told him to intercept all such letters; they were to be handed to you before they even went to my brother, if they ever did. I discovered that through Renaldi. I asked him as a personal favour to make enquiries. He discovered the truth. As the Pope's legate in this country no churchman would dare disobey him. The Prior had been warned right from the beginning that letters, possibly treasonable against the Queen, would be delivered to the Priory. He was to intercept them, hand them over to an officer deputed by the Queen and keep silent on the matter. That officer was you. That's how you knew where I was, what I was doing.' I paused to clear my throat. 'But one thing you overlooked. Stephen and I had made a pact. His only earthly possession was an amulet, a locket once held by my father, a memento of both our childhoods. If Stephen were to die before I did, his one last wish would be to return that locket to me. His Prior may never have known that I was the author of the letters. Moreover, any religious would obey the requests of a dying man.' I stopped to control the tears which welled into my eyes.

'Anyway,' I continued, 'Stephen died some weeks ago, probably not even knowing about the letters I sent or the danger I was in and the locket came back.' I dug into my wallet and brought out the battered bronze chain and its cumbersome pendant. 'Here it is, Simon! According to Renaldi, my brother died quickly of some chill but I suspect he lost the will to live years ago. He never really recovered from our father's death and may have wondered why his brother never wrote.'

Rokesley tried to rise but found he could not. He slumped back in his chair. His lips parted in a snarl of a grin.

'Clever, clever physician,' he said, 'and, if half of what you say is true, how can you prove it? What will you do?' His hands slipped off the table, he stirred and shook his head. 'I have drunk too much.'

'Oh, no, Rokesley,' I replied. 'You are dying. Your wine is laced with a deadly Italian concoction, but don't worry. Death will take hours yet. Your limbs and muscles will die but your mind will remain alive. You will be able to think and hear but not speak.'

I rose. Rokesley tried to stir but could not move.

'You have time to repent, Rokesley,' I said. 'Time to think. Time to plan. Time to pray. More time than King Henry had, more time than Ashby. More time than Trollope. More time than Cantrone. More time than my dear Blanche. God knows, more time perhaps than my poor brother, Stephen, whose letters you stole.'

Rokesley's mouth opened and shut, making only a gurgling sound as if he wished to retch and could not. I went and sat at the table opposite him.

'You deserve to die, Rokesley. You are an assassin. An angel of death. A destroyer of worlds. I feel no pity for you.' I glimpsed the look of hate in his eyes. 'You may think that I, too, am trapped, but I am not.'

I stood up and clapped my hands. The door opened and two figures entered. Gloucester, his face alive with excitement, and Gough, his lips twisted in a smirk of praise. I waved them forward.

'Master Rokesley, you know His Grace and His Grace's loyal servant, Matthew Gough.' I looked at them. 'You have heard everything?'

Gloucester nodded.

'Master Physician,' he said softly, 'you have told me more than I had ever hoped to hear.'

I stared back at him.

'I know you, Gloucester,' I said. 'I know your tortuous mind. If Clarence dies and he surely will. If Edward dies and he surely will. If his marriage is invalid and his sons bastards, then the crown of England will go to you.'

Gloucester just smiled. I looked down at Rokesley, his white face now covered with a fine sheen of sweat as the poison's grip tightened.

'Your Grace,' I continued smoothly, 'has agreed that I can leave the country. Once I am safely at sea, a friend who now holds Ashby's dreadful secret document will give it to you. I leave tomorrow in a cog bound for Boulogne.' I rose. 'Your Grace, I have your word?'

Gloucester nodded. He patted me on the shoulder, dismissed Rokesley with a flicker of contempt and, followed by Gough, quietly slipped out of my house.

So now I sit here, the candles guttering, writing this letter to a brother now dead whilst I watch my enemy die. So, why do I write this? Ah, only I see the jest. I am finishing what I began. This is my true confession but, above all, I know that the Prior at Aylesford, innocent of what is going on, will hold it until the Woodville bitch sends another man. Then she will know the truth. She will also know how Gloucester is a party to the secret and she can spend the rest of her days in terror. She should pray that her husband never dies whilst her children are still young. Gloucester is no Clarence. I suspect he will not be caught in her snares but go back to his beloved north and wait. Now all is complete. I know the truth. And what is it? King Henry was a saint. May he pray for me. The Woodville woman is a murderous bitch. Blanche is dead and so is Stephen.

And what does it profit a man if he gain the whole world but lose everything dear to him? The candles gutter out as does Rokesley's life. I will write no more. Farewell.

Conclusion
Letter 8

Hubert, Abbot of the monastery of Aylesford, to his father in Christ, Peter Renaldi, Cardinal Bishop of the Church of St. Priscilla and papal legate to the court of Henry VII of England. Health and Greetings.

Your Esteemed Excellency has always taken a keen interest in our house, especially the events some fourteen years ago when Brother Stephen Chichele was a monk here and the author of these letters (of which I send you a copy) was a physician in the court of Edward the Fourth. My purpose in sending these documents will become evident later, if it is not already obvious to you now. Surely your memory has been stirred? You must remember how many times you wrote to our house at Aylesford asking if we had copies of Chichele's letters. The abbot at the time, Father Hugo, always replied he had not.

Luke Chichele was brought here by the King's agents after being taken at Dordrecht in Hainault. The poor man did not know where he was, only weeks later did it dawn on him and then he just smiled quietly, crossed his arms, whispering 'Sweet Jesu, Sweet Jesu'. The letters we copied immediately as the Tudor wanted this matter fully investigated. Brother George did a skilful job. He ransacked Chichele's belongings and found the correspondence the King was looking for. Naturally, I was curious so I ordered Brother George to take a declaration from the Physician and copy out those letters we thought pertinent.

Four days after Luke's arrival in our house, the King sent down a young serjeant-at-law, Richard Foxe, an arrogant peacock of a man. I remember him well, standing in my chamber, legs apart, his cloak thrown over one shoulder.

'Father,' he demanded, 'you have spoken to Luke Chichele?'

'Yes,' I replied, resenting the royal

creature's patronising attitude. 'The poor fellow was quite witless. I could get little out of him.'

'And the letters?' the fellow asked.

I took a canvas bag from the great iron treasury chest of the monastery and handed it over.

'Do you know what these letters said?' Foxe asked, snatching the bag.

I shrugged.

'The doings of the world,' I lied, 'do not concern our small community.'

Foxe just stared back at me. Strange isn't it how times change but people do not? He reminded me of Rokesley, the murderer mentioned in Chichele's letters. The perfect royal official, the obedient courtier, who would probably cut his mother's throat if the necessary order was issued.

'You are sure about Chichele?' he asked. 'The fellow did seem bemused when we brought him here. We thought that returning to the monastery where his beloved brother had lived might clear his mind.'

I smiled to myself. Luke is a sad man, a

broken one but he still has his wits about him. Both I and Brother George had spoken to him. He is fearful of any royalty or those who serve them. He acted his part well yet I judge him to be of sound of mind as myself. Foxe seemed satisfied with my reassurances. He asked once more if there was anything else we had learnt and left, assuring me of the King's good favour. (As if I should be concerned with that?) I accompanied him back into the courtyard and watched him remount his horse.

'Master Foxe,' I asked. 'You brought the physician here in the hope that Aylesford might clear his wits. Why did you not take him immediately to some dungeon or seize the documents yourself?'

Foxe grinned and leaned down, patting the neck of his horse.

'The King,' he replied, 'knows Chichele was a famous doctor. His return to London may have been noted and tongues wag. The fellow still has powerful friends in the city. The same is true of the documents. The King wanted to make sure that everything was in order.' He stared coolly at me. 'Come, come, Reverend Father,' he continued. 'We both know what Chichele's letters contained and I am sure you have read them.' He wagged a finger at me. 'The King is quite firm on this matter. The letters touched on scandals best forgotten. He knows that Aylesford figured prominently in Chichele's life because of his brother. Now you know the secrets, you too are bound by silence. Tell others what you know and the charge is treason. You are, like me, Father, a servant of the King. And Chichele's secrets? They serve as padlocks for our mouths.'

I stared grimly back.

'And what about the physician himself?' I asked.

Foxe shrugged.

'The King is merciful. If Chichele stays here he may live out his days in peace. If he leaves,' the fellow smiled again. 'I leave that to your imagination, Father.'

Foxe turned his horse and I watched him canter down through the main gate and back to his royal master in London. I

255

returned to my own chamber, took out the copy of Chichele's letters and read it carefully. Truly, a tale of betrayal and great cruelty, yet one which brought divine retribution: within months of Chichele's flight to France, Clarence died mysteriously in the Tower. They say he chose his manner of death, a drunkard to the last, they drowned him in a vat of malmesey wine. Edward's affections did wander. Mistress Lucy and Mistress Shore both received marks of royal favour, physical and otherwise and with the passage of years Elizabeth Woodville grew more strident. Gloucester left the court and went north to York where he stayed, carefully protected by his own henchmen.

In the spring of 1483, Edward IV died suddenly, mysteriously, whilst boating on the Thames and Gloucester struck as venomous as a viper. The Woodville party was destroyed, the two young princes, Edward's sons, were taken into Gloucester's custody and he summoned Stillington to London. The Bishop only corroborated what Gloucester already knew: Edward IV's marriage to Elizabeth Woodville was invalid, his sons were bastards and, as no one born of illegitimate issue can succeed to the throne, Gloucester claimed the crown for himself. The two young Princes disappeared into the Tower and have never been seen since. Elizabeth Woodville was locked away under house arrest. Gloucester had himself crowned King Richard III but his reign only lasted two years. In the late summer of 1485 Henry Tudor landed at Milford Haven, brought Richard to battle outside Market Bosworth and destroyed him and the House of York for ever.

You might well ask why I tell you all this? Strange isn't it, the very day Henry landed at Milford Haven, the first person he wanted arrested 'for divers treasons and felonies' was our beloved Bishop Stillington? The Bishop was placed in the Tower and only released after he swore solemn oaths not to repeat slander against the King. Stillington, of course, broke his word. Two years later he was caught in a conspiracy against King Henry VII, taken prisoner and locked up in Windsor Castle where he eventually died. The Tudor King also insisted that all copies of Gloucester's declaration that the children of Edward IV were bastards were to be searched out, taken to London and destroyed. At the same time, he began his search for Chichele. God knows who told him, perhaps some Yorkist official who bought his life and honour with such information.

Now I ask you, why should the Tudor concern himself so much with Stillington, Chichele and other relics of the Yorkist reign? The answer is obvious. The Tudor's claim to the English throne is very weak. Who is he? Nothing but a Welsh adventurer of bastard issue. He hopes to unite the country by his marriage to one of Edward IV's daughters. He cannot afford to have any documents which casts aspersions against the Queen or, more importantly, his own children.

So, again I say, why do I tell you this? Out of a sense of anger. I was Prior when Luke Chichele was writing to his brother Stephen and, in his last letter, the physician made one dreadful mistake. He said that I was ordered by the Queen to intercept his letters but that is not true. The Queen, even the King, has no real authority in this monastery. The order was issued by you. Surely you remember? You sent Rokesley down. He told me, on your authority, that Chichele's letters contained 'matters seriously affecting both Church and State'. I was to intercept them and hand them, unopened, to Rokesley. I was also instructed not to breathe a word to Brother Stephen and to stop any communication between him and his brother. Thankfully, it did not occur. You also said that if the physician made any attempt to come to the monastery, I was to make up some excuse, bar his entrance and inform you immediately. I did so with a heavy heart for Stephen was a weak man in frail health. His brother's silence only worsened his condition and preyed on his mind. He fretted away his strength, gnawed by anxiety and muted reproaches against his brother. He died in my arms, begging me to send the pendant to Luke. I could not refuse a dying man's last request. Of course, when Luke Chichele received it, he realised something must be wrong and sent his messenger to you. You, artful as ever, neatly passed the blame on to the Queen. Of course, that royal bitch was to blame. You, however, deceived me and, in so doing, made me participate in something evil. You lied and used me. I asked the physician if, during his flight from England, any attempt was made to stop him?

'Yes, Father,' he replied. 'I fled the same night Rokesley died. The Queen did not yet know of my revelations but there were searchers along the Thames so Gloucester's men took me to an Essex port. Even there, searchers and spies were watching the ships. I only escaped because of Gloucester's influence. I have always wondered who alerted the Woodville so quickly.'

We both know, your Esteemed Excellency, that you did. I ask you, Cardinal, Papal envoy to England, what would the

Tudor think of a Pope's envoy being suborned by someone like Woodville and being involved in her sinister work? Henry Tudor would not be pleased to know that a Cardinal Legate had once been hand in glove with the Yorkist Queen? But, of course, you know the real danger. What would happen if the Tudor suspected you knew the scandal about his wife's birth and passed such information back to your masters in Rome to use when they think fit? Or are they your real masters? Or do you play a double game? In one of Chichele's letters he reports a conversation with the two French envoys, Lavalle and Roche. The physician, caught up in the dangers threatening him, failed to realise the significance of Roche's remark about Henry VI's sanctity: 'You opened his tomb at Chertsey,' Roche commented, 'and found proof of that.' But who told the French so soon about the tomb being opened? Gloucester? Never. Rokesley, Roche's murderer? I think not. The Prior of Chertsey Abbey would scarcely be their informer and Chichele never did, so that leaves you.

Whom do you really work for, Cardinal Legate? The College of Cardinals, the French court? I am sure you were interested in the canonisation of Henry VI but pushed the matter so as to fish in troubled waters. Hence your continued interest in Chichele's letters to our house. You are undoubtedly a spy and the Tudor would not like that. You can only imagine his fury if he discovered you may have told scandalous secrets about his wife, not only to Rome but his enemies in Paris. You must be more careful, just as you now realise why I am so confident in writing to you. I am sure you will remember this letter and be more than prepared to accede to any request I make of you.

Of Chichele himself what can I say? He stays in the monastery, content to act as one of our lay brothers. A constant source of help to our Infirmarian. He prays a lot, trying to free his tortured soul from his circle of pain and hate. He seems most at peace working in the herb garden, talking softly to himself. Once, I drew close and listened to his words. He was speaking to

Blanche and Stephen, whispering how he hoped they would admire his handiwork. Luke is often there, tilling the soil, talking to the dead. I once asked him if there was anything I could do. He just threw the trowel down and dusted the earth from his hands.

'Yes, Father,' he replied. 'You can pray that I will die soon.'

God forgive us all. Amen. Written under our secret seal at Aylesford — June 1492.

Author's Note

Most of the information contained in Chichele's letters reflects the known facts about the Byzantine intrigue which permeated the reign of Edward IV. The hostility of Clarence and Gloucester on the one hand and Elizabeth Woodville on the other is well documented. Clarence's treasons are described by the chroniclers and records of the times. Edward IV's secret betrothal to Eleanor Butler is also to be based on fact: Clarence was desperate to search the scandal out and Richard of Gloucester used it to debar his two nephews from the throne. Henry VII was equally vigorous in suppressing such scandal as well as searching out and destroying any documents connected with it. Both Henry VII and his son, Henry VIII, were obsessed with establishing their true claim to the throne of England and just as ruthless in crushing any challenge to it.

Clarence did die mysteriously, Edward IV's sons were debarred from the throne and Henry VII was equally assiduous in emphasising the legitimacy of his wife, Elizabeth of York. The Tudor's attempts to conceal scandal were not totally successful; during the reign of Henry VIII the imperial ambassador, Chapuys, repeated the rumours about Eleanor Butler to his master, Charles V.

Henry VI's sanctity seems well demonstrated. He may have been an ineffectual ruler but he was undoubtedly a holy man. In the 1930s Father Ronald Knox published the manuscript listing the miracles attributed to Henry VI. There have also been attempts to persuade the Vatican to canonise him. Henry's sudden mental collapse may well have been due to his wife's infidelity. I admit this is pure speculation although there were rumours about this whilst both Henry and Margaret were still alive. His corpse did bleed at St. Paul's and when it was transferred from Chertsey to Windsor (by no less a person than Richard III) it was reported that the body had not decomposed and gave off a fragrant perfumed smell. Antiquarians also relate that near the tomb 'were a cap and a dagger belonging to the King' and that the death wound was on the back of the King's head.

Of course, Luke Chichele, his wife Blanche and Brother Stephen are fictitious characters. They represent, however, many of the innocent, common people of England whose lives were caught up and destroyed by the great warlords of York and Lancaster.

We do hope that you have enjoyed reading this large print book.

Did you know that all of our titles are available for purchase?

We publish a wide range of high quality large print books including:
Romances, Mysteries, Classics
General Fiction
Non Fiction and Westerns

Special interest titles available in large print are:
The Little Oxford Dictionary
Music Book, Song Book
Hymn Bool

Also available f
Oxford U
Young Read
(large p
Young Read
(large p

For further inf
brochure, plea
Ulverscroft Larg
The Green, Brad
Leicester, LE
Tel: (00 44)
Fax: (00 44)